Mrs. Alexander

Found Wanting

Vol. II

Mrs. Alexander

Found Wanting
Vol. II

ISBN/EAN: 9783337047955

Printed in Europe, USA, Canada, Australia, Japan

Cover: Foto ©Andreas Hilbeck / pixelio.de

More available books at **www.hansebooks.com**

FOUND WANTING.

A Novel.

BY

MRS. ALEXANDER,

AUTHOR OF

" THE WOOING O'T," " A WOMAN'S HEART,"
" BLIND FATE," " FOR HIS SAKE," ETC., ETC.

IN THREE VOLUMES.

VOL. II.

London:

F. V. WHITE & CO.,
14, BEDFORD STREET, STRAND, W.C.
1893.

PRINTED BY
KELLY AND CO. LIMITED, 182, 183 AND 184, HIGH HOLBORN, W.C.
AND KINGSTON-ON-THAMES.

CONTENTS.

FOUND WANTING.

FOUND WANTING.

CHAPTER I.

"DUST TO DUST."

Mr. RIDDELL was more pliable than his daughter expected. She had prudently told him of Madame Falk's invitation in Ogilvie's presence, when they were dining with that gentleman at one of the pleasant restaurants on the Champs Elysées the same day that Madame Falk had left town.

"I suppose you would like to go?" said Riddell, who was sipping a glass of excellent Sauterne. "You fancy the joys of a rural retreat! Believe me you will be bored to death! Of course *you* find our good friend a congenial companion, I do not; which makes a great difference. You and I like women of a different calibre. Hey, Ogilvie?"

"I must say I find Madame Falk extremely likeable," returned Ogilvie, seeking May's eyes to read gratitude in them; " she is a bright, capable woman."

"Yes. I suppose she is, but there is no accounting for taste. Well, my child, I'll see what can be arranged. It might be a nice change, and do you good. *That* is enough for me."

"It is certainly very dreary for Miss Riddell to be left to herself completely."

"Yes," added May; " even Mademoiselle Perret goes away next week."

"I shall feel obliged to stay behind to take care of you," said Ogilvie.

May laughed.

"I am afraid your work is too important to be interfered with for so trifling an object," she said. " Well, dear father, may I write to Madame Falk, and promise to return with her when she comes?"

"I suppose I may as well say yes, as I generally do," returned Mr. Riddell, with an air of resignation, and they soon rose from table.

Mr. Riddell elected to sit and listen to some very lively songs at a café-chantant, while Ogilvie and May strolled up the beautiful avenue.

" It is a heavenly evening," he said. " Let us take a drive through the Bois. Your father will be quite well amused where he is for an hour or two. I told him not to wait for us."

May unhesitatingly accepted the offer. Ogilvie hailed one of the little open *fiacres* which abound in Paris, and they were soon *en route*.

It was an exquisite evening, and long dwelt in May's memory as the most charming experience she had till then ever known. Ogilvie seemed to lay aside all reserve, and spoke of his opinions, his convictions, his views and hopes, with a frankness that surprised and delighted her. Was it possible that a man so accomplished, so experienced, so superior, really intended to make a friend of her? This was indeed an honour. It seemed to stir her own intelligence, to fructify whatever seeds of knowledge and reflection

18*

she had been able to store up. With what flattering attention he listened to all she said, and seemed to find it very good! The delightful excursion was over but too soon, and on reaching the house they found that Mr. Riddell had not yet returned.

"And we might have had another hour!" exclaimed Ogilvie, in such a tone of genuine regret, that May coloured with pleasure.

"I am sorry too," she said. "But it was a delightful drive, and I thank you for it heartily."

Ogilvie smiled.

"The thanks are mine. I do not often find such a chance of exchanging ideas with my Egeria."

He lingered yet a moment under the porte cochère, and May, laughing at the idea of having any ideas to exchange, asked him to help in persuading her father to fulfil his promise to let her go to Madame Falk.

"A promise is a promise, is it not?"

"Yes, of course; only——" Here Mr. Riddell came up and made some remark about their being before him, adding :

"It is very good of you to trouble yourself with a chit like this girl of mine."

"That is all he knows about it. Eh! Miss Riddell?" returned Ogilvie with a good-humoured laugh, and then took leave of them.

When May had taken off her hat and lace cape, she found her father had lit the lamp, and was scratching calculations on one of the scraps of paper of which he kept a goodly store in a large envelope, the cover of some huge circular. Mr. Riddell never *bought* anything he could possibly procure in any other way.

"How long did Madame Falk ask you to stay?" he asked, looking up as May drew a chair, and brought her book to the light.

"She did not mention any time, but I am quite sure she will keep me as long as you are away."

"Ah! then of course you must return. I cannot do without my little girl," said Riddell, who seemed in high good humour. "Then, I think we will give Léontine the holiday she asked for. Then I shall have no mouths to fill for a fortnight except my own, and God knows *that* is easily done. Yes, my love! you shall go to our good friend— and enjoy yourself—if the kind of life pleases you."

"Thank you," said May simply.

"If my agents in London remit my interest to-morrow, I shall be able to start on Friday. I am sure I don't know what the fellows are about," continued Mr. Riddell in a lofty tone, as if his business alone were enough to occupy a firm. "I ought to have received it on Saturday."

The days which followed were very happily employed by May in her own preparations, which were of a very simple kind and un-avoidably limited. She was greatly exhilarated by the prospect of a change, as since she arrived from school in Paris she had never left it.

Mr. Riddell's reprehensible agents sent the cash as anticipated, and he made a little speech to Léontine, granting her the desired holiday, and was generally angelic.

"I am going to breakfast with Ogilvie to-morrow," he said on the Wednesday following their dinner with that gentleman. "He wants me to take up some work in London, something connected with translations, but I fear it is too mechanical for me. Besides, I am now so acclimatised to Paris that I do not know if I could live in the dense atmosphere of London. I fear it would not do. However, I shall hear all Ogilvie has to say. Really it is long since I met a man who suited me so well. He is highly cultivated, and quite on an intellectual footing with myself. I feel, too, that he appreciates me, which ordinary men do not. I am sure if I could assist him in his diplomatic work it would give me great pleasure. So, May, my love, you need make no provision for my breakfast to-morrow."

This happy mood continued next day.

Having dressed with his usual care, Mr. Riddell carefully locked up nearly all the loose money in his pocket, observing, " I shall only want a cab fare or so, and it is as well not to carry too much about with one. Good-bye, dear child. Let us have dinner half-an-hour earlier. I want to do my packing this evening, so as to have no hurry in the morning. Have *all* my things ready and laid on my bed before I come in." So saying, he kissed her brow, and went out.

The hours sped swiftly, for May was busy arranging and putting away things, being too unaccustomed to leave home not to make a mountain of a molehill. Then she had to write a joyous letter to Madame Falk, to announce her father's intended departure and her own readiness to start whenever Madame Falk came to town.

It was a warm day, and about five o'clock, feeling tired, she lay down on the drawing-room sofa, with an interesting number of *La Revue des deux Mondes*, and was almost asleep over it, when a sharp ring startled her, and as she sprang to her feet she heard Ogilvie's voice speaking to Léontine. The next moment he had crossed the threshold and stood looking at her silently. There was something in his face that struck her with sudden terror.

"What — what has happened?" she exclaimed, clasping her hands together.

" Your father has met with a bad accident,"
he said in a low, quiet voice.

" Ah! Mr. Ogilvie, tell me the truth—is he
—is he dead?"

" No—he is *not* dead, but in a hopeless
condition.   He asked for you—come with
me——"

" Where—where?" was all she could say.

" At the Hospital—not far.   I will tell you
all as we go along—do not lose time."

May, though trembling from head to foot,
promptly obeyed.   When she returned to the
salon, she found Ogilvie had spoken to Léontine, and had some wine on the table, which
he insisted on her drinking.

" After breakfasting together this morning," said Ogilvie, as they drove towards the
hospital, " we sat talking for a considerable
time, and as I had a visit to pay in the Rue
Tilsit, your father walked with me.   Not
finding the man I wished to see we returned
together and went some little way down the
Avenue Wagram.   Here your father bid me
good morning.   He attempted to cross the
road where it is steepest, and finding a large

omnibus coming rapidly upon him, he started forward to avoid it. His foot must have caught in something, or he trod on a stone which turned, for suddenly, to my horror, he pitched forward on his face under a large cart, with a pair of horses, which was coming down at a good pace. I saw it all. It was impossible to save him, he was under the horses' feet in a second, and sustained severe injuries."

" Is he—oh, is he suffering much ? " asked May, who was holding Ogilvie's hand with a nervous grasp.

" I think not—I hope not. He was only half-conscious, but he did say a few words to me and asked for you. It is a terrible shock for you, my dear girl. You have need of all your courage, but remember you have at least one devoted friend."

" If only he does not suffer," she murmured. " Is there no hope ? "

" I dare not encourage any," he returned. Then there was silence, save for a broken exclamation now and again, faintly uttered by May, until the hospital was reached.

May was too dazed to notice much till she was led into a small and rather bare room, exquisitely clean, where on a narrow bed lay a form, dimly visible through the coverlet, and a death-like face she knew well upon the pillow. She let Ogilvie's arm go and walked steadily to the bed-side. Was she too late? As she stood there with clasped hands, awed into composure, the dying man opened his eyes with a strange light in them, a faint smile flickered over his ghastly face, then the light died away, and the solemn stillness of everlasting rest settled down on face and form.

Ogilvie drew near, with a vague idea that May might fail and faint, but she kept quite still for a while, and then bent down to kiss her father's brow. Then the icy touch told her she had no father, and she drew back with a shudder.

Ogilvie drew her arm through his. " You can do no more for him," he whispered. " He had the comfort of recognising you!"

" I do not like to leave him," she whispered.

"Trust me. I have secured proper attendance, all that you can wish. You shall return to-morrow, if you desire it," said Ogilvie in a low tone. "Spare yourself! Leave yourself in my hands."

A painful, dizzy sensation seemed to paralyse May's heart; she did not lose consciousness, but she did not quite know what she was doing. She held Ogilvie's arm closely. She knew she was moving, then she felt fresher air on her brow, and found herself in a sort of vestibule or anti-chamber.

"Come, there is nothing more to be done," said Ogilvie softly. "I will take you home. Remember he is past all pain now, and you may rest. You have been a good daughter."

Then she was in the luminous darkness of the summer night, and felt the motion of a carriage, and knew that her hand was gently, tenderly held—that she was not alone.

Arrived at her home, she was tearfully embraced by Mademoiselle Perret, and overwhelmed by a torrent of ejaculations expressive of grief and affection.

"You will not leave her till I return to-morrow, said Ogilvie. " I take all care and responsibility on myself. I have been Mr. Riddell's nearest friend of late years. You will promise me," he continued, bending over May, who had sunk into a chair, " to try to sleep. I shall be with you early to-morrow, and I shall telegraph to Madame Falk. You can rest, for what can be done has been done."

Mademoiselle Perret volubly assured him that she would not leave the beloved, afflicted child for a moment, and sobbed and wiped her eyes till anyone might have supposed that *she* was the bereaved one. Yet the little woman was quite sincere in all this display of feeling.

With a lingering hand-clasp, Ogilvie left May to her kindly care, and then Léontine and Mademoiselle Perret persuaded their charge to go to bed, and the latter established herself at her side. It seemed to May that she could never sleep again, and even as she thought so the blessed balm of sleep stole over her, for the sudden and terrible shock had thoroughly exhausted her.

What varied and innumerable descriptions have been penned of the painful bewilderment, the intensified bitterness, with which those who have been struck down by sudden grief or loss, awake after brief oblivion to renewed consciousness of the blow—yet no words can adequately describe it.

To May it seemed when she opened her eyes the next morning that she realised for the first time the full meaning of what had befallen her. First and keenest came the sad certainty that her father must have suffered horribly. His haggard, drawn face suggested past torture, and she was not there to soothe or help him, and now she could never do anything for him again. Had she ever done enough? Had she not been impatient with his little foibles, and harsh towards what seemed to her his faults? What was she that she should judge?

Where is the eloquence that can send reproach to shiver through the heart, like the silence of death? Then she felt shocked at her own want of real grief. On the whole her father was kind to her, and she was cold to him, and irresponsive ; still he never seemed dissatisfied with her. At such a time, poor child, she would not allow herself to remember the isolation of her life with a man refrigerated by selfishness into an icy semblance of humanity, incapable of " giving out " anything, and stone-blind to truth. The death of such a father would be no heart-loss to any child.

Still, thought was very painful. May was thankful to get up and dress, to move about, often sitting down to collect her ideas, and wish that Ogilvie would come soon. What could she do without him ? She would leave herself entirely in his hands. But he was going away. Ah ! she must put *that* out of her mind, or she could not control herself. At last Ogilvie did come—she did not know how early he really did come. Then she felt stronger and more composed.

She begged him to take her once more to see her father before he was taken away for—— This Ogilvie gently but firmly re-fused, and persuaded her to give up her intention. Then he asked her about her own

and her father's relatives. Beyond her
mother's brother she knew none, and she
was vaguely aware that Riddell was not on
friendly terms with her uncle. Indeed, the
deceased always asserted that his brother-in-
law had behaved badly, nay infamously, to
him. It was significant of May's habitual
distrust of her father's statements, that she
did not think it necessary to mention this
estrangement to Ogilvie when he suggested
writing to this relative.

"When do you go to England?" asked
May when there was a little break in the
conversation. She spoke very low, with an
occasional tremor in her voice, which touched
Ogilvie profoundly—she was so calm and
strove so bravely to keep up and give as little
trouble as possible.

"I can stay long enough to be of use to
you," he returned, and stopped for a moment,
then with a slight effort added : "Your poor
father—in an interval of consciousness—
asked me to take care of you, to act as your
guardian, and I promised I would. I will
fulfil that promise, May."

" It was not right to lay such a burden on you, a comparative stranger," faltered May, struggling with the tears which would well up, chiefly because of the infinite comfort his words sent glowing through her veins.

"Am I a stranger in any sense?" he asked, stretching out his hand. "Do you hesitate to trust me?"

"Ah, no! I trust you as I never trusted any one before," she exclaimed, putting her hand in his. "Not even dear Madame Falk!" A smile, a kindly smile, passed over Ogilvie's lips as he held her hand gently for a moment.

"Then you accept my guardianship? I shall have but a short tenure of office. In less than a year you will be of age, will you not? Now I want you to go up to Madame Falk's rooms. The officials will soon be here to affix seals on all the receptacles which may contain papers, etc. So make your servant take up whatever you may want for a few days, until all the formalities are gone through. The *concierge* will no doubt give us the key. Indeed, everyone in the house seems anxious to do what they can for you."

May unhesitatingly obeyed ; she was only too glad to have so good a friend to obey.

She had hardly left the *entresol* when the men of the law arrived, and she was thankful she had escaped their presence.

As soon as she possibly could Madame Falk was on the scene of action, and, as usual, a potent and efficient help.

She at once took possession of May, and Ogilvie found an admirable colleague.

Then she arranged all about the mourning for the young orphan, accompanied her to pay the last tribute of respect to the deceased, and petted and coddled her *protégée* to her heart's content.

When at length, all legal regulations having been observed, May was free to examine what remained to her, and remove her belongings to Madame Falk's apartment that the *entresol* might be given up to the proprietor, it was found that beyond the quarter's income, just received, a few books and trifling personal possessions, such as clothes, a watch, and some ornaments of small value, Riddell had literally left nothing.

He had, after his wife's death, sunk all the property he could call his own in the purchase of an annuity, within which he managed by strict economy to live, and not a farthing remained for the support of his daughter.

"I wonder he could sleep in his bed at night when he thought of that poor, dear child!" cried Madame Falk indignantly. She was taking final counsel with Ogilvie, who was on the point of leaving Paris, respecting May's affairs.

"Yes, but he did not think of her," returned Ogilvie calmly.

"Now she is absolutely penniless," continued Madame Falk, "and I don't much see how she is to help herself; she has had next to no education. I might get her some writing or translations here and there, but it would amount to very little."

"Riddell has at least left next to no debt. In fact, the order in which he kept his affairs was admirable, and as we can give up the apartment and send off the servant, all expenses can be stopped at once," resumed Ogilvie.

19*

" Certainly May is more fortunate than many a fatherless girl, in having good friends," said Madame Falk. " That dear, kind creature, Mrs. Conroy, has sent me a handsome cheque for her use, and an invitation to stay as long as she likes, until she makes some plan for the future ; in short, Mrs. Conroy told me not to mention the cheque to May ; but that sort of delicacy is nonsense, so I did tell May, who is quite sensible, and greatly touched by Mrs. Conroy's kindness. I think she will go to Audeley Chase by-and-by, for Frances wrote such an affectionate letter she could not well refuse. But I can see she will never be content to live on charity. I wish she could get a position as companion or secretary to some rich old Englishwoman, there are such lots of them."

" Ah—yes, it is a good idea, Madame Falk. Poor May! it would be very dull for her," said Ogilvie reflectively.

" Women who have to earn their bread cannot be choosers. I should dearly like to keep her myself, but I cannot do that just at

present. I will take her away with me for a
fortnight's rest, and then see her off to Dieppe.
The Conroys will send someone to meet her in
London."

" It is well planned. People are rather
scattered just now, but when they begin to
gather together again, I shall look for some
elderly unencumbered lady, who requires care
and companionship," said Ogilvie, smiling.

" Pray do, Mr. Ogilvie ; and now let me
thank you both on my own account and
May's, for all your help, and all your goodness ! I do not know what we should have
done without you. And I confess, with
shame, that I thought you cold and selfish."

" You are right, Madame Falk. I am
both towards the world in general ; therefore,
what warmth I have for the very few who
interest me is all the warmer. May Riddell
is an excellent specimen of English girlhood
and interests me. Her father amused me,
and I had my reasons for cultivating him.
If I can be of service to the daughter, it will
give me , infinite pleasure. I trust that by-
and-bye some honest young fellow will see

what an admirable wife she would make. She is out, you say?"

"Yes, she has gone to put some flowers on her father's grave."

"Well, I shall take my chance of finding her to-night, or to-morrow morning, for the day after I must go to London. I have already over-stayed my time."

So they parted, mutually satisfied; indeed, Madame Falk felt quite enthusiastic about Ogilvie.

"He is really a good man," she thought, "and will be a most useful friend for poor, dear May! Should he happen to marry Frances Conroy, so much the better, as they will join in assisting my young protégé. And, of course, Ogilvie *must* marry money."

Madame Falk had some difficulty in mentioning her late father with anything like patience to May, so angered was she by the evidence of his extreme selfishness. To sink all he possessed for his own advantage during his lifetime, thus leaving his daughter totally unprovided for, seemed to her distinctly criminal. When the quarter's rent had been paid, the cost of the funeral and mourning settled, May would have been absolutely penniless but for Mrs. Conroy's cheque. "And thank goodness I have managed to get her a good rig-out," was Madame Falk's pious ejaculation. " She can manage nearly three months at Audeley Chase without any renewal." So she went cheerfully about her work, for all her sympathy and ready help, her counsel and direction, were mixed with rapidly-written articles on dress, fashion, sea-side gossip, the " on-dits " of the political and artistic worlds.

This had been a very busy day with Madame Falk, but it was not over yet. While solacing herself with a cup of tea, about five o'clock, a telegram was handed to her.

"Good heavens! This is a surprise!" she exclaimed as she opened it.

" What is it?" asked May.

" It is from my Californian editor. He arrived in Paris to-day, and wants me to dine with him at the 'Hotel Splendide,' and have a talk, as he starts for Russia to-morrow morning. Of course I must go. Shall you mind being left alone, May?"

" No, not at all! If I feel lonely I shall go and see Mademoiselle Perret. I do not dislike being alone."

" Perhaps not, but it is not good for you! I know you fret yourself!"

"Wonderfully little, Madame Falk. I sometimes think I have no heart."

" You will find that you have more than enough. I must put on my best bib and tucker. I do wonder what the man has to say to me. I hope he has some very advantageous offer to make!"

When Madame Falk had made up her packets for the foreign post, and, with May's help, dressed very carefully, she set out in remarkably good spirits to keep her tryst. May gave her a kiss, and a hearty "God speed," and returned to her friend's " Cabinet d'Etude," which she put in order, as far as she dared. Then she gave water to the flowers in the *salon*, and the plants on the balcony, and opened the Venetian blinds. The sun was now for some time off that side of the house, and a deliciously cool air came in through the windows. She sat down to enjoy the freshness, and to think. The first sharp impression of her father's death had worn off, and the sense of her extreme isolation pressed more and more upon her. She rather dreaded her visit to the Conroys, though she had firm faith in their kindness and constancy ; but she dreaded a plunge into a society of strangers, probably un-interesting strangers. Then the future ! Here the door-bell rang, and she went to answer the summons, for Adrienne had been left in the country with Miss Barton. At the door she found Ogilvie.

" May I come in ? " he asked.

" Oh, yes, pray do! Madame Falk has gone out, but I am so glad you have come."

" And I am not sorry to have a few words with you alone," he said as he followed her to the *salon*. " How sweet and cool it is here ! And—how white you look ! " sitting down beside her on the sofa near the window.

" But I am quite well, only a little tired. Do you leave Paris to-morrow, Mr. Ogilvie ? "

"Yes, and by a morning train, which accounts for my presence here this evening. And you will not be many days behind me, I believe?"

"I hope not. It will be very desolate when you are gone."

"Thank you. I am so glad I was of use to you. And you are going to stay with the Conroys? Do you think you will be happy there?"

"Yes. Frances is really fond of me. I know they are kindness itself, but I do not like to be a pensioner on their bounty, if I could do something for myself."

"Yes, it would be better. I confess to having an idea for you, but I must be in London to follow it up. Say nothing of this to anyone. Just leave yourself in your guardian's hands."

"Ah! that I will, most willingly. But do you really think you could find me some employment by which I could maintain myself?"

"I do, May. Leave it to me."

They talked on, till the twilight came

gently round them, of the past and future—
of thoughts and visions, with many a break
and pause.

"I should like you to be settled in
London," said Ogilvie, as he was bidding her
good-bye. "I shall probably be there for
some time, and I want to have my ward
under my own eye."

"And I should like it, too."

"Remember you keep me informed which
day you are to cross ; and what arrangements
have been made for your journey. Adieu for
a week or two. And never allow yourself to
feel desolate. Write to me whenever you
want me. Here is my London address." He
put a card on the table, held her hand in
both his for a moment, and was gone.

CHAPTER II.

"AT AUDELEY CHASE."

THOUGH still shadowed by the sense of awe and distress which had fallen upon her, with the sudden shock of her father's most unexpected death, May was fast recovering her tranquillity and courage.

She was always happy with Madame Falk, and the quaintness of their country quarters charmed her. The partners lodged in an old farm house of a better sort, to which was attached a mill, turned by a stream. It was situated in a valley a few miles from Rouen, and was altogether different from any place she had ever seen before. The valley was somewhat damp, but in the summer heat that did not signify. It was deliciously fresh and green. The sparkle of the water rushing over the wheel, the straight solemn rows of poplars which bordered the bye road leading to the mill, the poultry which at certain hours trooped from the yard across a corner of the orchard on one side of the house to the water, the fat, broad-backed, nearly white old horse that browsed under the apple trees, formed a picture of restful content, that made May long for the artistic power to put it permanently on canvas. Then, when she had a couple of hours to spare, Madame Falk would order the old horse to be harnessed to a very antiquated rusty calêche, and drive May into Rouen (she could put her hand to anything), where they enjoyed examining the beautiful old churches, the Palais de Justice, and other relics of old days.

It was a period of peace which enabled May to gather her forces for the battle which she told herself lay before her. Sometimes a sudden sense of her complete isolation would strike her with a shuddering fear: was ever any creature so divested of kith and kin as herself? Her only relative, her uncle, had written a very decided refusal to acknowledge her in any way, as he had been for years on bad terms with her father. Therefore, so far as family ties went, she was absolutely alone.

But she reflected, trying to rouse her courage, she had friends which are better than relations, and she had youth!

It pleased her to return to England. In truth, she had been far happier at school there, than she had ever been with her father, and she would be in the same country, perhaps in the same town with Ogilvie, round whom her hopes for future happiness were unconsciously gathering. Had any girl ever before had so delightful a friend, so wise, so steady, so considerate? Superior as he was in all ways, she could say anything to him, all her early timidity in his presence had melted away, in her instinctive recognition of the profound interest he took in her. Could any feeling, any attachment in the world, be so sweet, so satisfying, as the delicious friendship he had given her, and which he deserved from her! Life must always be full of charm while this lasted, and it would last.

A letter from Ogilvie was the only thing needful to crown this soft-grey dawn of a new phase in her existence but suffused with the rose of coming sunshine, and he did not disappoint her. It was not long, yet it said a great deal, and reminded her of her promise to let him know her movements. He also wrote to Madame Falk, telling her that he was going to the Highlands on a short visit to some relations, and should not forget his ward, as he had established the habit of calling her, should he fall in with any rich, halt, blind or maimed dowager.

The time for leaving the peaceful little valley came all too quickly. But if May dreaded the grandeur of Audeley Chase, she also longed to be in England, longed to be launched in some humble career, which would enable her to maintain herself; and that Ogilvie would find this for her, she never doubted.

She was very sorry to say good-bye to her good friends. Never had Miss Barton been so amiable. She had refrained almost altogether from acidulated remarks, and "Ivan," the beloved cat, whom Madame Falk had brought with her, as there was no one left in the *entresol* to care for him, had been very loving to the "favoured guest" at the Mill.

Madame Falk insisted on escorting May as
far as Dieppe, and seeing her safe on board
the steamer.

"You will have a long, tiresome wait, my
dear," she said as they stood on the deck,
having secured a berth. "I am afraid they
will not get off till two o'clock, and you will
not be at Victoria till ten to-morrow morning.
I wish you had someone with you! Make
up to that nice-looking, exceedingly English
old maid—I am sure she is an old maid—she
may be useful to you; are you sure you are
quite equal to calling a cab, and driving
across to the Midland Station? A porter
will get you one, don't give him more than
sixpence."

"I am not at all afraid, dear Madame Falk.
I speak my own language, and I have money
enough."

"That's right! Be sure you send me a
card to-morrow morning, and go straight away
to the Midland, you can get some breakfast
there. God bless you, my dear child! I hope
you will come and stay with me again. If
we could only find something for you to do in

Paris—but there! I must go back to the Town station. I'll sit in the waiting-room till the early market train starts for Rouen. God bless you, dear."

It was rather appalling being thus left alone in a crowd of strangers. This was indeed being cut adrift, and May could not keep back a few tears. But she was very tired, and following the advice given her by her friend, she partially undressed, and lay down in her berth, and dropped asleep before the steamer put off.

The night, or rather the early morning, was calm but foggy, and their progress slow. It was a dreary journey, but May met with no misadventure, rather with help and courtesy from her fellow passengers. It cheered her to hear English spoken on all sides, though a little puzzling, after being plunged for nearly six years in French. The sense of loneliness grew stronger as she approached the Metropolis, and she shrank from the idea of her solitary drive across the mighty town.

Now she was crossing the wide river. How wonderfully different everything looked from

what she was accustomed to, and how little
blue sky was discernible! Now the speed
was slackening, they were running under a
glass roof much blackened by smoke, they
were alongside the platform, a porter holding
on to the luggage; a few people stood about
evidently waiting for friends, a gentleman
came out from among them, some one she
knew; was it, could it be?—yes, it *was* Mr.
Ogilvie.

"Oh, how kind and good of you to come!
I am *so* glad! I thought you were in
Scotland."

"I considered it my duty to see you safe
off to Audeley Chase," he returned, handing
her out of the carriage. "You have had
a good crossing? You look quite fresh, and
less pale than when we parted," gazing at
her with the searching glance he rarely permitted himself. "Let us get your luggage,
and then you will breakfast with me at the
hotel."

"Thank you very much; but Madame Falk
said I was to drive across to the Midland
Station at once."

" Madame Falk did not know that I was coming to meet you."

" No, of course not," returned May, quite satisfied to stay.

" I have ordered breakfast, and I am very hungry," added Ogilvie, with a brief, pleasant smile.

To such reasoning there could be no reply. The luggage found, and consigned to the " Left luggage " place, Ogilvie led his ward into the hotel, where breakfast was laid in a private room, and consigned her to the care of a chambermaid, that she might make her toilette in comfort.

How grand and beautiful everything seemed to her! What a guardian angel Ogilvie was! Her return to her native land had, indeed, begun gloriously.

" Your train is at 12.50 from St. Pancras," said Ogilvie, as they took their places. " We may have nearly two hours to talk, which is not to be despised," and as he spoke it struck May that he was really very glad to see her, and that he looked younger than he had ever seemed before.

20*

Then followed a delightful repast. Led by
a few well-put queries, May described her stay
with Madame Falk minutely, dwelling warmly
on the great kindness of both cousins.
Ogilvie listened with an air of interest which
carried her on.

"Do you know," he said, when she paused,
" that you have rather remarkable descriptive
powers!"

"And do *you* know, Mr. Ogilvie, that is
very rude of a guardian to laugh at his
ward!" she returned, smiling.

"But I am not laughing," he exclaimed.
" I speak my real conviction."

May shook her head.

" Believe it or not, as you like," he added.
" Take some strawberries. Fruit is always best
at breakfast. And—are you sure you would
like better to live in England than in Paris?"

"In some ways, yes; though I should like
always to be near Madame Falk."

"Apart from that attraction, for you cannot have everything, you would prefer
England? Even London?"

"Yes, certainly. What I especially want

is to earn something for myself. I do not wish to live on the charity, even of the most generous."

"I understand that," said Ogilvie, thoughtfully.

"You said you thought you could help me." May hesitated a little over the words.

"I did, May. I have not forgotten. I still have the same plan in view, but you must leave it entirely to me."

"Of course I shall. I leave everything to you."

She raised her eyes as she spoke, and was struck by the sombre intensity of his.

"Your confidence is not misplaced," he said in a low tone. "Tell me how long are you going to stay with the Conroys?"

"I do not exactly know—as long as I like —two or three months, that would be long enough?" looking at him enquiringly.

"It would do very well," he said, answering the look.

"Shall you come to the Chase, Mr. Ogilvie? I know Mr. Conroy asked you."

"No, May; not this autumn. I have

many engagements." Since her father's death had drawn them so strangely near each other he had always called her "May."

"I suppose you are always greatly engaged?" she said.

"Well, yes; a good deal. Don't imagine, however, that my engagements are festive or social. They are chiefly hard business matters."

"Still, their reality must give them great interest."

"Profound!" returned Ogilvie, and grew suddenly silent.

The next moment he roused himself, and drew his companion on to speak of herself, her tastes, her ideas of the future, her few hopes; and though she was brighter than when he parted from her last, he could see how permeated her heart and soul were with the sense of her own insignificance and loneliness. He managed, however, to impress on her a conviction that she was of importance to him. He gave his address in Scotland, and begged her to keep him informed as to her life with the Conroys.

"I hope they will not have a very large party," said May, with a sigh. "I feel half afraid of a number of people."

"That is only the remains of the nervous weakness brought on by the terrible shock you have sustained. And, pray remember, your deep mourning gives you the right to stay in your room if any extra festivity is expected. But your own tact will counsel you better than I can."

"I am afraid not, Mr. Ogilvie," she was beginning, when she suddenly glanced at the clock. "Oh, is it not late—I must not lose the train."

"Do not fear. I have been keeping watch. I do not intend you to lose the train, I assure you. You had better put on your hat perhaps, though we have plenty of time."

Was it possible they had been talking for nearly two hours? Then came the drive to St. Pancras, it seemed wonderfully short.

"Oh, Mr. Ogilvie!" cried May, with a sudden spasm of memory. "I promised to post a card to dear Madame Falk, and I had almost forgotten—I am ashamed of myself."

"You can write one at the station. I will get one for you," said Ogilvie, smiling.

Having deposited his charge in the waiting-room, he went to see to the labelling of the luggage, and returned with the card, placed a chair for her near a huge blotter and a nearly dried-up ink-bottle.

"Before you write I must tell you that I am supposed to be in Scotland; my being here instead, is on account of some diplomatic business, and I must ask you to say nothing of having met me, either to Madame Falk or the Conroys."

May looked up a little surprised. "Oh! very well! I am glad you told me," then she quickly traced a few lines to the effect that she had had a very prosperous journey and now wrote from the Midland Station, whence she would soon start. "Will that do?" she asked, showing it to Ogilvie.

"Perfectly! you write a remarkably firm hand. It is not the sort of writing one would expect from you. I always remark that to myself, when I get your letters."

"I don't suppose I am firm, though,'

returned May reflectively, as she drew on her glove.

"You do not know what you are yet," said Ogilvie smiling.

"Perhaps I never may; but I am not a child, Mr. Ogilvie."

"No, that you are not, you are every inch a woman; all you lack is experience, and that will come soon, *too* soon. I don't imagine that even in your infancy you were a thoughtless child. By-the-way, do you think you could translate? If so, I think I could get you some work."

"I could only translate French, which I imagine everyone can read now, and I am not sure I could translate into really good English."

"We shall see. Now I must let you go! Your journey will not be much more than four hours. I am, I assure you, quite sorry to part with my—may I call you my pupil?"

"You may indeed, you have taught me a great deal," looking gratefully into his eyes. Ogilvie smiled.

"Perhaps it is a case of reciprocity," he said.

"Ah, that is not likely," returned May, shaking her head.

"Time is up, I must get you some papers to help you through your hours of imprisonment." He led her to a first-class carriage.

"But, Mr. Ogilvie, I was to travel by second——"

"You are to do what your guardian desires," he interrupted, "you will have the carriage all to yourself; unluckily this is a slow train, but, 'per contra' very few going as far as Kingsford travel by it."

He disappeared, but soon returned with various illustrated publications. Then he held her hand for a minute. "I shall see you before long, and mind you let me know your impressions of English country life."

"You may be sure I will! Good-bye! thank you very much for your great kindness."

The guard's whistle warned him to step back, and the next moment she had lost sight of him, and was fairly plunged into the unknown.

May did not open her papers for a considerable time, she was too much absorbed by her gratitude for Ogilvie's great goodness in taking so much trouble about her. How differently she felt on this second stage of her journey from the desolation which over whelmed her when she parted with Madame Falk the night before! she felt "strong and of a good courage" now that she was so assured of Ogilvie's thoughtful friendship. He would take care of her, in a way she most desired, by finding her work. There was that about him that was expressive of power, of a reserved force which no one could exactly measure. "But even on him I must not lean too much, I must not burden him in any way; a certain degree of equality is the essence of friendship! But how little I can do!—yet I can learn. I wonder what plan he has in his head for me? He has one I am sure! I am fortunate to have such a friend!"

She was indeed amazed at her own good spirits, and a little ashamed of them.

In truth her father was no real loss to her. The incident of his desertion of her in her dangerous illness had so soon· given her the key to his character, that it brought a discordant note into their intercourse which she could not away with; she could not shut her eyes to his selfishness, his petty untruthfulness, his sham existence! and now, having utterly forgiven the painful past, the kindest course was not to think of him at all.

It was a glorious afternoon when she reached her destination. Glowing golden sunshine bathed the landscape; the trees and fields had put on their richest, deepest green, the roads were dry and white, and May, wearied out with dust and heat, felt suddenly revived when she recognised Frances and Mr. Conroy on the platform as the train came to a stand at the little station.

"Ah, May! delighted to see you! 'Had a tolerable journey?" cried Mr. Conroy in joyous tones, as he shook hands heartily with her.

"So glad, dear May!" said Frances,

embracing her with unusual warmth. "You look so pale and tired! What luggage have you? Tell Peters, he will attend to it, and will drive up to the house at once."

Instructions having been given to an elderly groom, Frances put her arm through her friend's, and they passed through the station to the space behind, all persons raising hats, touching caps, or dropping curtseys as the great Miss Herbert Conroy passed, a new experience for May.

A pretty low phaeton and a pair of beautiful brown ponies were waiting for the heiress and her friend, the reins held by the smartest of grooms, while a boy held a fine grey hunter, evidently aged, who pricked up his ears as Mr. Conroy approached. He asked affectionately for Madame Falk, and made further inquiries as to May's travels. "You know we thought some friends of Esther's would have been travelling over with you, or we would have sent some one to meet you."

"Thank you very much. I got on very well indeed ; you know I speak the language," said May, smiling, and she stepped into the little carriage.

"I am bound in an opposite direction, we'll meet at dinner; you are our only guest at present."

Frances took her seat, the ponies pawed the ground impatiently, the groom jumped up behind, and they wore off at a rattling pace, so fast indeed that May held on very tightly. "Do you always go so fast, Frances?"

"Oh, the ponies are very fresh, they will settle down presently."

The country was rather flat, but rich, and, in the direction towards which they were going, thickly wooded. It struck May that there was an air of cheerfulness and comfort about the cottages and hamlets, by which they passed in their six-mile drive, that seemed different from the aspect of the country round Paris, of which she had a few rare glimpses; but she was a little dazed by the complete newness of everything.

Audeley Chase was a fine old place. That portion near the much-patched and added-to original Tudor house was perhaps too much embowered in trees, but at less than half a mile's distance began an open space of heather and fern, grass, rocks, and occasional clumps of trees, which was the real Chase. Immediately round the house were mossy green lawns and pleasure-grounds, kept to a pitch of perfection which astonished the young visitor—conservatories were fitted in to several of the angles of the quaint old house, and a peacock strutted on a terrace on which the principal rooms opened.

"To think of three people having all that great house to themselves!" thought May as they stopped at the wide flight of low steps leading to the open entrance door. Yet the whole place was more lovely and delightful than grand or stately.

Within there were numerous passages richly carpeted and abounding in carved oak, bronzes, china, old pictures, and all that could delight the eye. Through one of these May was led to Mrs. Conroy's private sitting-room, a charming apartment with delicate pale grey walls, on which hung choice landscapes in water-colour; it opened into a conservatory and thence a few steps led into the grounds.

Here the lady of the house received her guest, with her usual gentle kindliness, touched by the tender sympathy she felt for a young creature so curiously denuded of all family ties. " I am very glad to see you, my dear child, and I hope you will stay as long as ever you like," she said, kissing her brow. " Frances greatly needs a young companion, and I don't think she cares for any girl except yourself. Now Frances, take her to her room and order some tea there; I shall not expect to see either of you till dinner time."

May was deeply moved by this kindly greeting, she could hardly keep back her tears or command her voice.

" She needs rest, Frances," she added in a low voice.

" Yes, no doubt; she never was strong! Come, May dear!"

At last Miss Conroy—after administering tea, and a good deal of information touching her own doings in the past and plans for the future — left her friend to rest, and for some time May kept perfectly still on the sofa, from which she could see through the open window, over the lawn beneath, to the background of beautiful foliage which shut it in.

She had never seen so charming a bed-room before. The chintz hangings, the elegance of the furniture, though simple and light, the long glass, the endless appliances for comfort and convenience, the delicious scent of flowers from within and from without, seemed to her too much beauty and luxury for any mere mortal. And there were many houses like this scattered through beautiful England! Musing on the extraordinary difference between her own life and that of her friend, she gradually fell into a light sleep.

From this she was roused by a loud but not unmelodious ringing; at the sound Frances entered the room.

"It is the dressing bell," she said. "I hope you have had a nice sleep? I will send Hortense (you remember my maid, Hortense, in Paris?) to unpack your things; she was so pleased to hear you were coming."

" Oh, thank you, Frances! I can do every-thing myself."

" You must let Hortense help you this time. It is not necessary to make much of a toilette, we are quite alone and will be till next week."

" I have very little of what you call toilette to make," said May.

" Quite enough, I daresay—I will come for you when I am ready myself."

Dinner was served in a large dining room, like a baronial hall, full of carved oak furni-ture, curious blue china, pictures and all kinds of suitable decorations.

The Squire took in his wife, leaving the young ladies to follow arm-and-arm. May thought how well suited Mr. Conroy looked to be at the head of such an establishment, and withal there was a homely heartiness in his kind attentions and hospitality, that the humblest might be at home with him. Dinner over, the master of the house proposed that they should take their coffee on the terrace—much to May's satisfaction.

" You see 1 can have my cigar out there

without offence," he said, with a nod to May, as he put his wife's lace shawl round her. "I know Madame does not like tobacco in her dining-room—though she is obliged to put up with it when some young fellows are here."

"This is pleasant, hey, Miss Riddell?" he resumed as he watched the curling smoke when they were settled in comfortable basket-chairs round a small table, which had been set forth by the butler, assisted by a magnificent "Jeames." "You couldn't do this in Paris, charming as people find it?"

"No, indeed," exclaimed May. "The wonder is to me that you can ever tear your-selves away from so delightful a home."

"Ay—so do I, that is quite my idea. There is no place like the Chase to me."

"Yes, it is sweet, I know," said Frances, "and for a while it is very well, but one's faculties grow paralysed here. There is no mental friction—no mental life. I must say that much as I love the Chase I could not support existence without a visit to the Continent—a peep at Paris every year. I

21*

think I like Paris better than London, I seem
to know my way about better."

" Well, I do not like any town except for a
short spell," returned the Squire. " I don't
care for Frenchmen—very good fellows, I dare
say, but I don't understand them. By the way,
you saw Ogilvie just before he left Paris ? "

Mrs. Conroy looked warningly at her husband—she feared the mention of his name
would bring back too painful associations
—but May was glad to speak of him, and
answered steadily :

" We saw him nearly every day. I cannot
tell you how good he was, how thoughtful !
I do not know what I should have done without him, nor Madame Falk either. She was
like a mother to me—but then she knows
French people chiefly—now all the people in
authority, French and English, knew Mr.
Ogilvie and attended to what he said."

" True. He's a very rising man—ought to
go into parliament—a right good fellow too !
glad he was so useful to you, my dear. I
wish you would ask him to come here for
a little shooting on his way back from

Scotland " (to his wife). " He is in Scotland, isn't he ? "

" He was going there, he said, the last time he wrote to Madame Falk," replied May, a faint colour rising in her cheek at the prevarication.

" Is he not Scotch ? " asked Mrs. Conroy.

" His family is. But he himself is a thorough English gentleman," said the Squire.

" May," said Frances, " am I selfish and unreasonable if I ask are you too tired to try over some of our old songs ? I liked your accompaniments so much ! "

" Yes, Frances," put in her mother, " you are both. I think vocal music must jar——"

" No, dear Mrs. Conroy," interrupted May. " I am quite ready to play for Frances. It has done me so much good to come, but to-night I am dull and tired and——"

" By George ! you shall go to bed as soon as the light is gone," cried the Squire.

" I am too thoughtless ! " said Frances. " Come, May, we will stroll round the lawn, there is a pretty peep of our old church through the trees at the other side."

CHAPTER III.

"SOME LETTERS."

"Glendaroch, August 17, 18—

"DEAR MAY—

"It is nearly a fortnight since I heard from you, let me have a report of your proceedings soon. Your last two letters have been as brief as my own. Pray remember that although I am too overdone with correspondence to write at length to anyone, that is no reason why I should not like to read what you have to say.

"Very glad you are happy with the Conroys, they are excellent people; I am sorry I cannot accept their invitation. I am obliged to go on a special mission to Marseilles, and shall get very little shooting this season, as I must hurry away to meet H. in London on the 23rd. I shall be in town again in Oct. certainly, and hope to arrange the plan I have spoken of, for I am sure your present contentment is only provisional. Any news of Madame Falk?

    " Always your sincere friend and guardian,
                " PIERS OGILVIE."

           " Moulin des Bois, près Rouen,
               August 20, 18—
" DEAREST MAY,—

    " You *are* good to write so often in return for my rare scattered scraps. I assure you both Sarah and I enjoy your accounts of life at Audeley Chase; to me they are specially interesting, as I know it well; some of my happiest childish days were spent there. Oh! so long ago! But my memory of it does not present me with the picture of perfection you describe. In my day, except for a narrow ring round the house, the grounds were a wilderness, the gardens an unpruned mass of vegetation, the house an old curiosity shop of faded furniture and worn carpets. I cannot say how it rejoices me to hear that the dear old place is restored to more than its pristine glory, and still more to know that, with a large fortune, Herbert secured so sweet a wife. Certainly few men

deserved one so well.   He is the best man I
ever met, and after him comes Mr. Ogilvie.
I wish Frances would marry one of the
various 'desirables' you mention as hovering
round her.   Matrimony would cure her of
her fads, which must be funny.   She is rather
a puzzle to me.   She is certainly kind and
considerate for others, yet, we must admit, a
good deal taken up with herself.   Wealth
and indulgence have spoiled her just a little.
You see we still stay on here.   I do not
know when I had such a long delightful spell
of the country; the reason I can stay is that
I made great friends with a delightful old
advocate to whom I was able to do a good
turn (a journalistic turn, you understand).
He is one of the Directors of the Chemin de
L'ouest and he has given me a pass, so I can
run to and fro to Paris, which is a great help.
My advocate knew Flaubert and others, his
intimates, very well.   He talks delightfully
about them.   He rides out sometimes (on
such a droll pony) and takes coffee with us.
Sarah makes a great deal of him, and you
know how difficult *she* is !   We go back to

Paris the first week in September, and shall always have a '*gite*' for you when you want to come. I think I could find something for you to do, but take my advice, stay where you are until I can take a good look round, for employment is not easy to discover. I have almost forgotten to say I had quite a long letter from Mr. Carr. He writes from— where do you think? Warsaw! He seems roaming about very indefinitely. He had only heard of your poor father's death just before, and appeared greatly shocked. He enquires very kindly for you. Sarah sends her love, so would dear Ivan if he knew our language. By-the-way, Sarah hopes you will not adopt extravagant habits and ideas, she thinks her countrymen the greatest spend-thrifts on earth.

" Good-bye, dear child,

" Always your attached friend,

" Esther Falk."

" Rue C——.

" August 23, 18—

" Beloved child,—

" How faithful you are, to remember

your poor little old friend, amid the spendour of your surroundings. It is a true pleasure to read your charming letters and see with your eyes the new scenes you describe. I am indeed rejoiced that you have found so excellent an asylum, but, my little one, you must not count on it as a permanent sojourn. Human nature is frail and variable, few possess the constancy which would make a dependent, however charming and estimable, welcome for always; therefore dear child let me offer you a little word of counsel. If among the gentlemen who frequent the hospitable château where you dwell, one seeks you in marriage (which is not improbable, befriended as you are by the most distinguished family of the neighbourhood), do not refuse him; unless indeed advised to do so by one who knows him on account of his want of fortune or his indifferent character. An established house, a legal protector, are enormous advantages; though one be small, and the other more or less plain, it matters little. You have none of the boldness which shows itself in the generality

of English young ladies; you are incapable
of wishing to be in love before you are
irrevocably united to your husband. Then
the sense of common interest, and an
indissoluble tie, gives each interest in the
eyes of the other, from which a tender
friendship will, in well - regulated minds,
assuredly arise! Think of your friend's
advice, my little one, and pardon my
frankness.

"For myself, my small affairs go not so
badly ; at present my pupils disperse themselves to the four quarters of the earth, but I
feel sure of several who will return, and have
hope of many new ones. I have felt
encouraged to take a sleeping chamber on
the second floor. It is very suitable, with an
alcove, and a stove on which I can even cook
a little dish, as I hope my dear child will see,
for you will come to Paris, will you not? and
perhaps bring M. le Mari with you? Think
always of the future, ma petite chatte. My
health has been miserable, alas! nervous
attacks, the result of a too delicate organi-
zation rendering me at times incapable of

movement; and as you know the concierge
of this house is a woman of the worst
disposition; *intrigante* to the nails of her
fingers, insolent, false, everything that is
worst.   She irritates me in a manner not to
be described, and I suffer.   Heavens! how I
suffer! but I cannot permit myself to say
more.   Those ladies at No. 13 have not
returned, and a new family, the widow of a
late official in the Ministère de Finance, has
taken your entresol.   Alas! the tears come
to my eyes when I pass the door.   Adieu, my
sweet young friend,

" Your devoted,

" THERESE PERRET."

This last effusion came in a huge square
envelope, with a fifteen centime stamp, and
May had to pay five pence for it; but what
pleasure it gave her!   What pleasure all
three letters gave her!   To be so kindly
remembered and wished for, why should she
trouble about her lonely position when she
thus lived in the hearts of her absent
friends?

"Is that a warrant from a secretary of
state?" asked Mr. Conroy, who as usual
distributed the letters at breakfast - time,
noticing the size of the foreign envelope.

"No! It is from my good friend Mademoiselle Perret! You have seen Mademoiselle
Frances?"

"Yes, I remember, a very little woman,
but an excellent musician; she had been a
pupil of Garcia's, I believe, and her style is
thoroughly Italian."

"It is! She is such a dear good soul, you
will be amused with the epistle by-and-bye,
Frances."

No more was said then, for there were
several visitors at table, and May waited to
re-read and enjoy her letters until she was in
her own room.

There had been for nearly a month a
succession of visitors, chiefly men, staying in
the house, and the results were less agreeable
to May than might be imagined.

According to the ethics of Romance, the
attractive, graceful dependent ought to have
proved irresistible to the male members of

the party, and thereby excited the wrath of the heiress towards one who ought to have been insignificant. In this true tale this was not the case. The simply dressed, quiet, pale girl in deep mourning, though graceful and lady-like, was unmistakably a nobody; taken up, no doubt through some charitable, or humanitarian whim by the fanciful little heiress. She was therefore passed over, not discourteously—for men are scarcely ever rude to inoffensive women, be they ever so lowly—but with a perfunctory politeness quite perceptible. The golden youths who came to shoot, and try their chance at Audeley Chase, soon found that she did not understand their shibboleth, while her conversation seemed "flat, stale, and unprofitable" to them.

One or two of the older men did not dislike taking her in to dinner, for she listened patiently and politely to their talk, and, when it had any, seemed to perceive their meaning.

Then she played Miss Conroy's accompaniments unoffendingly, when that young lady chose to tickle their ears, a "sweet obligingness" on her part for which they were not quite as grateful as they might be.

Indeed, one man, Monti Fane, otherwise Lord Montague Fane, an æsthetic, high art, " greenery yallery-Grosvenor Gallery " sort of youth, who played tuneless rambling rhapsodies on the violin, and did not care for hunting or shooting, also found her accompaniments very useful and quite intelligent, so much so that he had an indistinct idea (none of his were very distinct) that he might start her in London as a fashionable accompanist, and reap the fruits thereof. Monti Fane was a very well-known man, and quite an authority, among a certain set of wealthy fashionable dowagers of rank, on matters of taste and art, literature and the drama.

May did not care much for the society which gathered at the Chase during this period, and of the two she liked the women less than the men. There was something hard about them that made her shrink—they followed their own pleasures so boldly—they were so occupied with manly sports and pursuits—that she felt even less at home with

them than with their male companions. Yet
now and then little gleams of good nature,
touches of kindly pity for the poor, shone
out, that startled and puzzled her. Was
their hard indifference then only a disfiguring
mask, which a troop of malignant fairy god-
mothers compelled these young Princesses to
wear? If so, it was the worst infliction that
could be devised.

How thankful she felt that Frances had
taken up a different line! She was fanciful—
and showed in her fads a great want of
common sense — but she was kind and
womanly. So May stayed contentedly with
Mrs. Conroy, read to her, walked with her, or
drove with her, while Frances and the other
young ladies walked with " the guns," or rode
" matches" with those men who could be
induced to forego the birds.

The Squire good-humouredly offered to
teach her to ride, but May declined; she had
not had nerve enough to attempt it, and urged
as an excuse that she was too old to begin.

The morning May had received the letters
given at the beginning of this chapter, some

of their visitors, Mrs. Gray and her two
daughters, were to leave by a comparatively
early train. Frances went with them to the
station.

Returning, she asked May to come to the
music-room.

" With all this outdoor exercise," she said,
" I neglect my music, and I really do not
know how we should get through the evenings without a little music. Monti Fane
wants me to try that duet of Verdi's with a
violin second ; I should like to try it over, as
they are all out of the way."

" Very well. Why don't you sing those
Russian songs we worked so hard at last
spring, Frances ? They are very charming,
and might amuse our rather unmusical
audience."

" I am afraid I do not quite remember how
to pronounce the words, May."

" I am sure I have not forgotten ! I thought
of them by day and by night then, I was so
anxious to know them thoroughly—they are
ground into my brain. You sang them so
well at Madame Zavadoskoï's."

" Well, I think I did—and what pains Mr. Ogilvie took to teach me. It was a very pleasant time that season in Paris. I was so sorry Mr. Ogilvie could not come here on his way south. He is really very *distingué*, and a very rising man. I wish——"

" What ? " asked May, smiling as she paused.

" That he took my opinions and tastes more seriously. He was scarcely civil, May, and really—I am not silly—nor a mere baby ! "

" No, certainly not ! " returned May, yet not altogether without hesitation. She longed to be able to explain to her friend that she had no natural power of selection, and put the same energy and seriousness into the discussion of a conjuror's tricks as into the gravest question of politics or morality—that she tried to dabble in everything. But these are the kind of truths that no woman (or indeed man either) can tell another, and live !

" I suppose," she went on, " that Mr. Ogilvie has seen and read and done so much, he does not think a girl—like you or me—

has any right to an opinion." But while she said it, a pleasant, soothing recollection of his patient receptive mode of listening to what she herself had to say, swept through her mind. Certainly there was a strong sympathy between herself and Ogilvie. Secure in the friendship of such a man, she might well be indifferent to the neglect of others.

" It is extremely narrow and unjust," said Frances, after a short pause, " and I regret his narrowness the more, because he has been so good to you. How hard it is to find anyone who is really consistent."

" I suppose it is, but don't you think a thoroughly consistent person would be rather formidable ? "

" No ; why should he be formidable ? "

" Oh ! because—because, I don't know, only I *feel* it."

" My dear May, you are very illogical. Let us begin—would you like to play over the accompaniment first ? "

" Yes, I should, and you could read the words."

Then a very interesting practice ensued. Miss Conroy remembered the music well enough, but the meaning of the words, and the pronunciation of some of them, had escaped her.

How vividly the sweet, sad, peculiar airs brought back the first days of her acquaintance with Ogilvie to May's mind and heart, how astonished she was when it first dawned upon her that he rather liked to talk with her, and took the trouble of arguing with her and explaining things to her. Then she was aware of a sudden intense desire to see him and hear his voice again, and it would be quite two months, probably more, before she could expect that delight! He had spoken of October, and what he said she firmly believed. Would he write from Marseilles? Well, she must not be foolishly impatient. He would do what was best and wisest.

"May, I don't think you are attending," said Frances in her serious, measured way, "those notes are all wrong."

"Forgive me! I did forget what I was doing. Let us begin again."

This time both song and accompaniment went well.

"I fancy Monti Fane will be charmed with these," said Miss Conroy. "He will want to play them on the violin."

"A violin accompaniment would be a great improvement," returned May. "Are you going to meet the guns?"

"No, I have no one to go with me."

"I will, if you wish?"

"Thank you, dear, but they will be too far by this time," said Frances. "I will drive with my mother to-day and come back to receive Mrs. Montgomery, she comes just in time for dinner. You will be amused with her, she is a widow, and very rich; she was a beauty too, but has a fight not to look *passée*."

"If one has had beauty, it must be very trying to let it go," observed May, as her fingers wandered over the piano. Miss Conroy did not answer at once, she was leaning on the piano, and gazing at vacancy.

"I imagine Mr. Ogilvie would be very hard to please in a wife," she said abruptly.

"Yes; so hard to please, that I doubt if he will ever find one to suit," returned May laughing.

"Still, I do not fancy he will remain an old bachelor, and my father says he must marry money."

"It is impossible to say," was the cautious reply.

"Do you think he would be a severe or kind husband?" asked Miss Conroy.

"Who can tell? He is a kind, true friend, but does it follow he would be a kind husband? I do not think he is the sort of man who would be as happy married as unmarried."

"Ah! there is the luncheon-bell, we must not keep mother waiting, while we conjecture respecting what we can never know. Will you have a good practice while we are out, May? You really play very nicely, but you ought to be more diligent and persevering, dear; nothing is done without work."

"Quite true, Frances. I will follow your advice."

Mrs. Conroy was looking a little pale and

fagged. She was far from strong, and her chest was delicate. A succession of visitors for any considerable time was too much for her, for she was too sympathetic and unselfish a woman not to give herself trouble about them. Nor could she well bear the winter at Audeley Chase. The place was rather cold and damp, and this was one reason why the Conroys frequently wintered abroad.

" Frances," she said, when luncheon was half over, " I have had a very kind invitation from Emily, that is Lady Lyndthorpe, to spend part of October with them. They have taken that sweet place near Falmouth, which they had the winter before last. I think it would be well to avoid the fall of the leaf here."

" I am sure it would, mother! and my father would be able to enjoy his hunting all the better if he knew you were comfortable and out of harm's way."

" Yes, and perhaps the Leslies might come and stay with him. Mr. Leslie is so glad to get a little hunting, and *she* is a great ally of Mr. Conroy's." The conversation continued on the same topic. Mrs. Conroy was a good deal taken up with the project, and proposed taking a house near their friend's if one could be found.

She seemed pleased to have her daughter to act as her charioteer, indeed May had always noticed that the gentle mother seemed to long for a little more of her child's society.

Luncheon over, May sat in one of the windows of the hall, looking at *The Times*, till Mrs. Conroy and Frances appeared ready to go out, and watched them drive off. After standing uncertain for a few moments, she took her large shady hat, and wandered out into the woods just outside the grounds. Here she sat down on a mossy ridge beside the path which traversed them, and gave herself up to thought.

For the first time since she had been left, as she believed, to Ogilvie's guardianship, a little anxiety respecting her future began to gnaw at her heart. If Mrs. Conroy and Frances were going on a visit in October, she would be cast adrift without a home, and nearly penniless, save for a very few pounds, the remains of Mrs. Conroy's kind gift. She had not enough even to take her back to Paris, nor, if she had, could she quarter herself on dear Madame Falk.

With sudden force came back the sense of her loneliness, her poverty, her helplessness, for she was but ill equipped to win her bread, and, even if she could, she must not live on charity. Between her and all the ills of life there was but one plank, Ogilvie's friendship, and that might not exactly fail her, but could he create work for her, find her a home, raise up a protectress when hundreds, nay thousands, were seeking what she wanted? Thousands infinitely better fitted than herself, with more to give in return for what they asked. Still as she recalled his quiet, resolute face, the calm decision of his movements, the suggestion of reserved force in every word and gesture, a reassuring conviction that whatever he planned, he could carry out *if* he chose, and that he *did* choose she could not doubt. She longed to write to him and tell him that the ground on which she now stood was crumbling under her feet, but was she not worrying herself uselessly? Was Ogilvie a man likely to be false to a promise, forgetful, inconstant? No! As she recalled his look, his voice, she determined to banish these uneasy anticipations, and believe in his loyalty as she knew she could in her own.

Having quieted her heart by a strong effort of her will, May started for a short walk through the wood nearest the house, and having enjoyed the sunset through the trees, returned to have a good long practice before Frances and her mother returned.

It seemed as if Ogilvie was to be the subject of conversation that day.

When Mrs. Conroy settled herself in her favourite chair, a little tired with an un-usually long drive, May offered to read aloud a fascinating novel, an offer gladly ac-cepted. Frances, who rather despised novels, went away to give directions to the gardener, and May went on with her lecture, occasion-ally stopping to make a comment on the characters, till the sound of horses' feet and the crunch of carriage wheels upon the

gravel, told that the expected visitor whom
Frances had gone to fetch was approaching,
while the distant sounds of shots presaged the
return of the sportsmen.

May slipped away to her room, glad to be
out of the way, and to do a little necessary
needlework.

When all were assembled before dinner,
she found the newly-arrived guest to be a
tall woman, stately and elegant. To May's
eyes she seemed by lamplight still fair and
young, with great dark, lustrous, oriental-
looking eyes, and a mass of soft, dusky, curly
hair. Her beautiful white throat appeared
bare down almost to her waist, so long was
the open V of her corsage, while a similar
opening at the back seemed to stretch
from the "mique" far below her shoulders.
She was exquisitely dressed in delicate black
lace over mauve, and ornaments of opals and
diamonds sparkled here, there, and everywhere. She was standing in one of the
windows, though the lamps were now lit, as
the dinner hour at this season was eight, and
all the men of the party were gathered round

her. May took her usual place partially behind Mrs. Conroy, and looked with sincere admiration at the handsome widow, amused with her airs and graces.

When dinner was announced, she fell to the lot of a good-humoured, frosty-faced, sporting old bachelor, who had a pretty little place in the neighbourhood, and who generally was assigned to May when he dined at the Chase. They were opposite Mrs. Montgomery, who was on her host's right.

"She's a stunner, ain't she," said May's cavalier, seeing her eyes fixed on their neighbour.

"She is very beautiful," returned May in immense admiration.

"Wait till you see her ride!" continued Major Harding. "There's nothing she can't do. Hunts, shoots, fences, does everything well, and talks—thirteen to the dozen."

"She must be very clever," said May.

"Ay, that she is! She doesn't let the grass grow under her feet," ejaculated the Major, and then addressed himself seriously to his dinner. May, not being so much engrossed in that occupation, gave her attention to the beauty opposite, who was talking to her host in a strong and certainly not musical voice, to May's regret, as she wanted the object of her admiration to be completely charming.

"Yes! We hadn't a bad time at Glendaroch," she was saying when May caught her words. "We made heavy bags every day, and—oh! by the way I met a friend of yours there, that is a man who seemed to know you very well—Mr. Ogilvie! I met him some time ago, when I was travelling in Hungary, where he made himself very useful to me when I was in a difficulty. Rather an interesting man, and a rising one. Old Brackley of the Foreign Office told me it was a great pity that he had not entered the high diplomatic line. I don't know how he came to be mixed up with the commercial side of diplomacy. He is ambitious too. His thorough knowledge of Russian makes him very valuable to the Foreign Office. They say he is to go to Japan."

This announcement sent a chill to one

listener's heart. Ogilvie at the other side of
the world would leave her friendless indeed!
" But he would not leave her in ignorance of
such a project, no!—" May thought, " he
was far too kind, too considerate for *that*."

She felt a little dazed, however, and only
heard indistinctly the rather continuous talk
of the brilliant widow, who discussed many
things with a tone of decision, as if from her
judgment there was no appeal.

After dinner there was more talk, and an
animated game of billiards, but no one
seemed inclined for music, so the Russian
airs remained unsung.

May was much amused by the performances
of Mrs. Montgomery, who seemed to take
possession of the place and the command of
every one in it.

" Who is the girl in black ?." she asked
Mrs. Conroy, somewhat audibly. " I don't
think I ever saw her before."

" Probably not, she has chiefly lived in
Paris, where we made her acquaintance.
Frances is very fond of her; she lost her
father a few months ago, poor thing."

" Ah! to be sure, she has the air of a picturesque orphan in an old - fashioned romance! She might be made a good deal of, but no doubt she will marry some curate or country lawyer."

"I trust happily in any case," returned Mrs. Conroy, smiling at the summary manner in which the superb widow dismissed the insignificant topic.

May, however, said a quiet good-night to Frances, and went away early to her room.

When safely shut in there she wrote a short note to Ogilvie, telling him that Frances and her mother were to leave home in October, and asking his advice as to what she should do. She felt more relieved when this was finished and ready to put in the post-bag next morning.

" He will not have left London without letting me know," was her last waking thought.

Meeting Mrs. Montgomery at breakfast next morning was somewhat disenchanting. The want of youthful freshness and smooth-ness of complexion, scarcely observable at night, was visible in the morning. She was in what she termed her shooting dress and looked more sporting than charming.

She and her numerous followers started soon after breakfast with much hubbub of talk and noise of dogs, carrying Frances with them.

May was happy enough with Mrs. Conroy all day, for the shooting party had luncheon sent out to them at some distance. Yet she could not quite banish the sort of uneasiness which had disturbed her since she had heard of Mrs. Conroy's autumn plans.

Her faith in Ogilvie was justified. By the second post, which reached Audeley Chase about seven, came a few lines from Ogilvie, who said:

"You will receive a letter with this or soon after, from a relative of mine, an elderly, unmarried lady, whose sight is failing. She wants some one to read and write for her. She will offer you a miserable salary, for she considers herself poor. I do not! Accept however. I shall tell you more when we meet in October. Greatly pressed, but yours ever,

"P. OGILVIE."

It was dated the night before. So he had been thinking of her and writing to her when she was writing to him. This communication sent her down to dinner with a tinge of colour very becoming to her, and gave her life enough to play Frances' accompaniments with spirit and expression.

Next morning brought her the following, which was addressed

"To Miss RIDDELL, AT HERBERT CONROY'S,
      "ESQUIRE, AUDELEY CHASE.
   "MADAM,—

      "Being in need of a person who can read aloud intelligibly, and write a fairly good hand, as my sight is indifferent, my kinsman, Mr. Piers Ogilvie, has recommended you to fill the situation as companion, as he tells me you were committed to his care by your late father. As my circumstances are somewhat limited I can offer only a small

salary, but you shall have a comfortable
home, and liberty to worship according to
the doctrine in which you have been brought
up. As it is weary work writing to and fro
about particulars, I suggest your coming to
stay with me for one month to try how we
like each other, commencing from the 25th
of September. Should we agree, your salary
shall begin from that date.

"I am, Madame, yours faithfully,

"EUPHEMIA MACALLAN.

"16 Granby Road, Kensington Gore, W."

CHAPTER IV.

"MISS MACALLAN AT HOME."

THIS was not a very attractive or amiable letter, nevertheless May made up her mind at once to accept Miss Euphemia Macallan's offer. Ogilvie's few emphatic words were quite enough for her; still, she would not write in reply until she had spoken to Mrs. Conroy and Frances respecting it.

For an opportunity to do so, she must wait till the following morning; as it happened there was a large dinner-party that evening, and May had begged leave to remain in her own room, as it seemed hardly fit that she should appear at so large a party not quite three months after her father's death.

She quite enjoyed the silence and repose of her lonely evening, and plied her needle while her thoughts wandered away into the future.

This Scotch lady (May supposed she must

23*

be Scotch) seemed rather hard, but no doubt
she would not make herself very disagreeable
to a companion, backed up, as May was, by
so powerful a protector as Ogilvie must be.
He had evidently planned the engagement for
her, and perhaps the formidable Miss Macallan might prove interesting and malleable
on a closer acquaintance. At any rate, May
reflected, she would be in London, where she
would have opportunities of seeing Ogilvie
occasionally, if—he did not go to Japan or
any other end of the earth! *That* was a
possibility she did not like to contemplate!
But she must accustom herself to expect it,
for, however attached friends might be, they
were never linked like—— She arrested her
own thought at the words which suggested
themselves, and a smile dimpled round her
lips, as she remembered Ogilvie's objection
to marriage. Indeed one could hardly
imagine him a married man. He seemed too
much an abstract of intelligence, worldliness,
and good breeding, to be amenable to the
common laws of ordinary existence — to
endure the homely happiness of comfortable

married life. Certainly he was very good to
his self-imposed ward. There was nothing
cold or indifferent in his real kindness, yet
his words and manner were calm and serious
enough for "a potent, grave and reverend
signor," but she felt (why, she could not have
said) that there was a curious affinity between
them, something in the tone of his voice
when he spoke to her, in the touch of his
hand, on the rare occasions when he took
hers, that communicated a strange, delightful
sense that her presence gave him pleasure,
that he could talk to her without restraint,
that he trusted her unstintingly, and not
undeservedly, for she never repeated a
syllable he said to her, nor let any eyes save
her own rest on what he had written. Yes,
whatever Miss Euphemia Macallan might be,
however miserable the pittance she offered,
she (May) would at least try to live with
her, and get on with her, for she felt that
such was Ogilvie's wish, and that he would
not let the effort be too painful. Occupied
with such-like dreams the evening passed
rapidly, she heard the carriages drive

away, and before she began to undress
Frances tapped at her door to say good-
night.

"I think you have had the best of it, May!
We were rather dull; dinners in the country
generally are!"

"I have been very comfortable and con-
tented," returned May. "Frances, are you
going out early to-morrow?"

"No, I am quite tired, and Mrs. Montgomery does not want to go out either."

"Then I want to consult you and Mrs.
Conroy about my small affairs."

"Why, what has happened?"

"It is too late to discuss anything now. To-
morrow will be quite time enough, and you do
look pale and fagged." With a friendly
good-night the girls parted.

*   *   *   *   *

Next morning was very wet, with occasional
gusts of wind, and the only lady visitor (for
May was considered one of the family) took
her breakfast in her room.

"Come to mother's boudoir, May,"
exclaimed Frances, as soon as the gentlemen

had left the breakfast-room. " May has something wonderful to tell," she added.

" No, nothing wonderful ! " said May smiling.

"What is it ? " asked Mrs. Conroy, as soon as she settled herself in her favourite chair beside her work-table.

" Please read that," was May's reply, handing her Miss Macallan's letter.

Frances, too, read it, over her mother's shoulder.

" What a disagreeable, cast-iron person she must be ! " was Mrs. Conroy's comment, when she finished the epistle.

" And not at all well-bred," added Frances.

" Really, May, my dear, I should not accept the offer," continued her mother. " You may as well stay on here."

" But Mrs. Conroy, though you are so very good, and make me so happy, I cannot continue living on your bounty, on charity —for it is charity, when you do nothing to earn what is given, even as generously as you give. I shall be in the way at some time or other, for instance when you go from home on a visit! It is so difficult too for a girl who, like myself, has no particular requirements or accomplishments to find employment, that it would be very unwise of me to refuse this offer."

" Perhaps so," said Mrs. Conroy reluctantly ; " of course your principle is right, May."

"Then," urged May, "this lady's proposition that we should try each other is very fair, and above all, Mr. Ogilvie, in a few lines which I had last night, advised me to accept. So, dearest Mrs. Conroy, I have quite made up my mind to try life with Miss Macallan."

"Then there is no more to be said," replied Mrs. Conroy, who was re-reading the letter, " but I must say this does not give me the idea of a person who is easy to live with."

"I hope she will let you come to see us sometimes!" exclaimed Frances. "I hope we shall be in Town after Easter, and see you often. Ah! here is my father."

" Well, what are you in conclave about ?" asked Mr. Conroy coming in as she spoke.

"May wants to go and seek her fortune," said Mrs. Conroy, smiling and handing him the letter.

"Gad!" he cried when he had read it. "This is a regular go-to-meeting old cat! Don't go near her, May! She'll put you on half-rations, and you are only beginning to get into condition as it is; she'll ring a curfew at eight or nine o'clock, and put out fire and light, and get the last farthing's worth of work out of you! Stay where you are, till you find something with a sunnier aspect than this skin-and-bone employer."

A brisk discussion ensued, but May was not to be turned from her purpose, and even Mrs. Conroy admitted that it would not perhaps be wise to refuse what Ogilvie had taken the trouble to find for her.

"Well, well!" cried Mr. Conroy. "You may try it. She can hardly manage to starve you to death in a fortnight or three weeks, for if you don't think it will suit, you need not stay the whole month out! Just come back to The Chase, and we'll find a corner for you. Now, 'Madame'"—as he generally called his wife—"I want you in the study for another consultation."

So the council broke up, and May remained unmoved.

Writing a proper reply was not a difficult task, and then she had the pleasure of inditing a letter to Ogilvie, apologising for troubling him with the one which had crossed his, thanking him for all his kind thoughtfulness on her behalf, and assuring him she would do her utmost to please his kinswoman; then she paused, longing to ask: "Is it true that you are going all that weary way to Japan?" but she held her hand. It would be too great a liberty to question him as to his plans or intentions. Were she face to face with him, she might mention having heard Mrs. Montgomery say so, but she must not write it, it would be presuming on his goodness and indulgence.

Ogilvie answered her letter promptly. Life with Miss Macallan would be, he feared, somewhat dull, and at first she might not seem attractive, but she was less formidable than she looked, and a curious mixture of habitual stinginess with occasional fits of generosity.

"It is, however," he continued, " the beginning of independent life for you, and better things may come.   At least, you may be sure of consideration and politeness, as my ward, and I hope to see you from time to time.

" I wish I were to be in London, to introduce you personally to my cousin, but I leave for Marseilles to-morrow, and fear I shall not return until the second week of October."

May was quite content.   It would be delightful to see her guardian, as she considered him, now and then ; she could expect no more.   At any rate, if the seas did not roll between them, she could always turn to him in any time of trouble.

Still, it would be a wrench to part with her kindly friends at the Chase—especially Mrs. Conroy—whom she found more really companionable than Frances.   If Miss Macallan were only like Mrs. Conroy, she could live with her for ever, and feel like a daughter to her employer.

The beginning of September was wet and stormy, the succession of guests for shooting ceased, and Mrs. Conroy began to long for the softer climate of Cornwall.

"It will soon be here—I mean the twenty-fifth," said May, one wild afternoon, as they sat round the tea-table in Mrs. Conroy's favourite drawing-room, where a cheerful wood fire was blazing.

The Squire had ridden away to Kingsford in defiance of the weather.

"Is your courage oozing away as the hour of trial approaches?" asked Mrs. Conroy, smiling; May had evidently spoken out her thoughts.

"I am afraid it is, Mrs. Conroy," she returned. "I have hitherto been so fortunate in the kindness and sympathy of my friends, that the idea of a plunge into cold water, such as I cannot help fancying awaits me, is a little shuddery."

"Well, you must remember it is only experimental, you must not martyrise yourself even to please Mr. Ogilvie!"

"I am sure he would not expect you to do

so," said Frances, who was slowly stirring her tea in a thoughtful manner.

" Is he in London ? " asked Mrs. Conroy.

" I think not ! He told me to write to the club if I wanted anything, but that was nearly three weeks ago, and I have had nothing to write about since," and May sighed.

In truth, this break in their correspondence made her courage sink to zero.

" Quite wise of you, dear," returned Mrs. Conroy, " never trouble a man with unnescessary letters ; they are easily bored."

" I wish I had some work to do—or work I could do, in Paris, and could live with Madame Falk ! She is always so busy and so bright, and we are so accustomed to each other ! " resumed May.

" This new acquaintance may prove much better than you expect, May," said Mrs. Conroy. " Now I have been arranging things in my own mind. Suppose, Frances, that we all start together on the 25th or 26th, and as we must stay two or three days in London to shop, May, who must want winter things, shall stay with us, and we'll do all our business together. Write to Miss Macallan, May, and ask her to let you postpone your arrival till the 30th, that will be time enough, and we'll see you safe into the lion's den."

"Dear Mrs. Conroy! how good you are!" cried May, the colour coming to her cheeks, the moisture to her eyes. "It is indeed a kind thought, but I do not want to shop. Madame Falk promised to have my last winter's cloak dyed, and——"

"My dear child! permit me to judge for you! You are going to be independent, if working for a pittance can be called independence; allow me to enable you to start fair. I have a commission on that score from Mr. Conroy, who is, I assure you, quite concerned at your leaving us."

"Yes, May, you must do as mother wishes," added Frances, "and when we are in Town I will take you see the Geological Museum. I always regret your indifference to that most interesting science."

So after a few grateful, agitated words, for she felt it hard to express all she felt to these

good friends, May retired to write, as Mrs.
Conroy wished, to Miss Euphemia Macallan.

That lady replied by return that Miss
Riddell's suggestion suited her very well, as
one of her servants wanted a holiday, and
would therefore be absent until the 29th, and
it was as well that the visitor should not
arrive till the following day.

* * * * *

It greatly softened the regret May felt at
leaving the charming house where she had
been so kindly sheltered, to have the friendly
owners for her companions, at any rate for the
first stage of her journey into the unknown.

Mr. Conroy, with his usual care for his
women-kind, escorted them to Town, and
remained to see his wife and daughter safely
started on their journey south-west before
returning to the Chase.

To May, the days spent in a grand West
end hotel were more bewildering than
pleasurable.

She was almost frightened at the sums
expended by Frances and her mother in what
they considered necessaries for the winter,

and had great difficulty in persuading Mrs. Conroy to let her choose sufficiently simple and inexpensive things for herself.

At last the dreary day came when she must part from all she had ever known, and plunge into an entirely new world.

It was a bright, crisp day, and Mrs. Conroy observed very pleasantly, that she was glad to see that the sun shone upon her young friend's enterprise.

May could hardly smile.

She had sent Ogilvie a few lines to announce her slight change of plan, to which note he had not replied. Was he—now that he had fulfilled his promise of finding occupation for her—was he going to relax in his care for her? She would not think of anything so dreadful—so annihilating! But her kind companion noticed that she looked white, and that her lips quivered, and reproached her for her lack of courage.

Granby Road was an old-fashioned street, leading south from Kensington Gore; and on the east side were solid, red-brick houses, with tall, narrow windows, and big knockers on the hall doors, also wide entrances and stairways. Opposite, were much more modern, semi-detatched villas, of the perky, pretentious order, with gardens in front, some of them well-kept, and others not—for the place was going down—the lower end was already in the hands of the destroyer, and about to be merged into " Mansions " not " in the skies," but next door to them, in fashionable altitude, *i.e.*, South Kensington.

" It seems rather a dull situation," said Mrs. Conroy, as the carriage stopped opposite an evidently well-cared-for abode, with delicately clean muslin curtains, resplendent brasses, wherever brasses ought to be, and beautifully whitened door-steps.

The door was thrown open by a neat damsel in a large muslin cap and a dandified white apron. Miss Macallan was at home, Mrs. Conroy and May descended and were shown into a rather dingy but spacious dining-room, covered with a worn turkey carpet, and furnished with a row of very solid, leather-covered chairs ranged against the wall, an " uneasy " arm chair at either side of the black fire-place, a knee-hole table in the window, a big funereal sideboard of dark mahogany opposite, and a large dining-table in the middle.

From one of the uneasy chairs, as they entered, up rose a tall, angular figure, clad in a silk garment of shot green and crimson, surmounted by a tall head, a pasty, freckled face with high cheek bones, pale grey, stern eyes, a rather grim mouth with an obstinate-looking long upper lip and a bony chin; these were enclosed within a stiff, reddish-grey, sausage-like curl at either side, each kept in its place by a monstrosity called a side comb, above which a white lace cap with pendant lappets completed the toilette.

As she stood silent for a moment, Mrs. Conroy began in her gentle, well-bred tones: " I have taken the liberty of accompanying my young friend, Miss Riddell, to see her safe into your hands."

"I'm sure you are varra guid," returned Miss Macallan, with a mechanical widening of the lips intended for a gracious smile. "I've been expecting you this hour past."

"I am sorry to be late," said May falteringly.

"It is of no consequence," returned Miss Macallan, with a wave of the hand. "I am glad to see the young leddy. Indeed, any friend of my kinsman Ogilvie is welcome to me."

"Thank you, very much!" said May, somewhat comforted.

"And pray have I the pleeshure of speaking to Mrs. Conroy?" continued Miss Macallan, whose broad Scotch we shall in future leave to the reader's imagination.

"I *am* Mrs. Conroy, and beg to thank you for your courtesy in leaving Miss Riddell with us for a few days longer. We too have the pleasure of knowing Mr. Ogilvie, and I hope when we return to Town to call upon you, if you will permit me."

"Certainly! I shall be extremely glad to make your acquaintance." A few more civil speeches and Mrs. Conroy took her leave.

May clung to her a little in the hall, and kissed her cheek with unusual demonstrativeness.

24*

" Don't worry yourself, my love," whispered the good-natured matron. " I think she in-tends to be very civil, and that means a good deal ; write soon, and tell Frances *every* thing. Good-bye, my dear child." Another moment and the carriage rolled away and May, feeling more utterly desolate than she ever did before, while she kept back her tears by a desperate effort, returned to the solemn dining-room.

" Ah, well, come and sit you down a bit," began Miss Macallan, " it will soon be time to light the gas and then Rebecca will show you your room. I'd go myself, only I am a sufferer from rheumatism, and these bright crisp days it is just more than I can manage to go up and down stairs more than once a day. You have the room next to mine ; it's a nice comfortable apartment and if I should want you in the night—quite con-venient."

" Thank you ! " returned May, a little at a loss how to reply. " Of course you must not think of toiling upstairs with me."

" You are in very deep black," resumed

the hostess. "I suppose your father is not that long dead?"

"Not more than three months," said May, sadly.

"Eh! that hasn't given you much time to get accustomed to the lone business, and my cousin Ogilvie will have been his nearest friend, since he left you to his care?"

"They were a great deal together, and Mr. Ogilvie has been wonderfully good to me. I can never be grateful enough to him."

"He was always weel intentioned," remarked Miss Macallan meditatively, "though whiles he had a hard way with him."

"I thought so too, when I met him first," said May——

"Eh?" cried Miss Macallan keenly, her head a little on one side like an incarnate note of interrogation. "Then you did not know him when you were a bairn?"

"No," returned May, suddenly put on her guard by her interlocutor's tone, "only since I grew up."

"May be you come from the north countrie

yourself — Riddell is a good old Border name ? "

" My father was quite English, though I have heard him say his people originally came from Scotland, but I know no relations, as I have lived chiefly in Paris."

" Well, all things are mixed with mercy ! " said Miss Macallan solemnly. " It's a blessing my kinsman took you out of the place before they made a Papist of you."

" I assure you, no one ever tried. The people I lived amongst were not inclined to convert their neighbours."

" Which does not speak very well for their religious convictions," returned Miss Macallan sternly. " Those who have been blest with a knowledge of the Truth, ought to be ready enough to speak a word in season."

May preferred to accept this species of rebuke in silence.

" I suppose then," resumed Miss Macallan in more cheerful tones, " Mr. Ogilvie manages everything for you—your money matters and all ? "

" Exactly, and I am glad to think that he

has not a difficult task," returned May smiling. She meant that, as far as money went, there was nothing to manage. Her hostess, however, construed her words differently.

" Eh! it's something to be thankful for when a man leaves what belongs to him of this world's goods clear and straight instead of all through other! And so you wish to live in London, eh ? "

May began to weary of this cross-examination—moreover, though he had never enjoined reticence upon her in so many words, she felt that Ogilvie did not wish her to be outspoken so she made an attempt to release herself.

" I only wish to live where I can do something to earn my own bread, Miss Macallan, and I hope you will find me of some use. Now if you will allow me, I should like to go to my own room and unpack my things before dinner."

" You seem a wise-like young lady," returned Miss Macallan, " and I'll ring for Jessie—but I hope you are not too much accustomed to fine ways, and late dinners. I have just a chop or a slice of cold ham to my tea. It's less costly, and more wholesome, so I hope you won't mind."

"Me? Oh, no. I have just come from rather a grand house it is true, but my own home was homely enough!"

"I am glad to hear you say so—for I am a homely person myself—and there's no doubt you are the sort of girlie I wanted."

Here a sort of replica of Miss Macallan herself—only a little taller, a little gaunter, a little greyer, and crowned by a muslin cap with a goffered border, entered the room saying in a rather high-pitched voice:

"Did you ring, mem?"

May could hardly believe that anything so antiquated and rigid could answer to the soft, youthful name of Jessie.

"You'll just take the young lady up to her room, Jessie, and undo her trunk for her. You'll show her the chest of drawers and hanging press."

"I couldn't just very well empty the wardrobe and big chest of drawers now, but——

"Oh, I daresay I shall have quite room enough," cried May. "I have very little to

put away," and she followed Jessie upstairs,
leaving Miss Macallan in a brown study.
What object could her " Cousin Ogilvie " have
in befriending a young, penniless girl, who
wanted to earn her bread? He, whom she
had always respected as a " hard man "? Not
but what he had always kept up with her.
She was his mother's cousin, and had been
very friendly with the late Mrs. Ogilvie, who
married above her own station. In truth,
Ogilvie had been very fond of his mother,
and Miss Macallan had been more with her
than any other friend or relative. The
shrewd Euphemia was very proud of her
successful kinsman, who had a very curious
amount of influence over her. And she
devoted a good many half-hours when " it
was just waste " to light up yet a while, or
while she was jolting in an omnibus to Stagg
& Mantle's on a remnant day, to the consideration of what possible motive could actuate
Ogilvie. At last her imagination settled a
delightful succession of cause and effect.
" That cunning chiel," Ogilvie, had some
private knowledge respecting Miss Riddell's

right to some large fortune, at present seeking
an owner, and so soon as he had made her
his own he would prosecute her claims, and
in Ogilvie's hands, with his opportunities, a
large fortune would soon become colossal.
It was a beautiful vision of love and money,
quite captivating to her imagination, and the
Scotch imagination is a good stout, serviceable
article, capable of stretching to a large
extent.   It was many a day since such a
romantic possibility presented itself to the
mental ken of Euphemia Macallan.

"And I'll give her no chance of saying I
didn't treat her well, and give her of the
best," was the distinct resolution which
closed this spell of reflection, or rather this
piecing together of possibilities and pro-
babilities.

"Is that you, Jessie?" hearing a quiet,
measured tread in the hall.

"Yes, mem."

"Come here, Jessie."

Jessie obeyed.

"And is the young lady satisfied with her
room?"

" She didna say to the contrary, mem."

" She did not look as if she wanted a fire ? "

" A fire ! " in a piercing tone of astonishment, " and we not yet intil October ? What for should she want a fire ? "

" Well, Jessie, she's a young lady who has been accustomed to every comfort, and will again, no doubt, and Mr. Ogilvie would be sore vexed if we let her want for anything."

" Eh, mem ! she seemed well content. Indeed, she is a pleasant young leddy and speaks verra soft and kind. She noticed the grand big bed—it's more than she is accustomed to, I'm thinking, for she laughed and said, ' I shall not be able to find myself in so large a bed as that to-morrow morning.' "

" Yes," returned Miss Macallan with justifiable pride, " it *is* a handsome bedstead, and what's more, there's a real down bed on it. Now Jessie, my woman, just make us some cream scones for our tea. It will be a treat for an English lassie, only, as it is not a company night, make them *without* the cream, Jessie — she does not know — she'll never miss it."

"Verra well, mem," said Jessie, and departed kitchenwards.

Altogether May felt less wretched than she expected to be, when she descended on hearing a gong making as much noise as if it announced a banquet instead of high tea. Miss Macallan was something quite new to her—her quaintness amused May immensely, and her hostess's evident anxiety to be civil and conciliatory convinced her that her good friend and guardian had insisted on her being well treated.

The sepulchral dining-room looked a little more cheerful when the gas was lit and the table spread, and Jessie's cream scones (the cream omitted by " particular desire ") were excellent, in spite of the omission.

Miss Macallan was a continuous talker, and during the evening meal kept up a constant stream of questions respecting the domestic arrangements at Audeley Chase—the habits and customs of the proprietors, and the probable cost of the establishment.

Tea over, May, anxious to be up and doing, offered to begin her duties by reading aloud.

"You'll be too tired!" said Miss Macallan, "and I have nothing in the house but last week's *Scotsman*."

"Have you no especial book on hand now?"

"No. I have read all that are in the house, except the Rev. Angus McCrae's new volume of sermons, and I am no very pleased about it."

"Are they not well written?" asked May, trying to seem interested.

"You see, this is what I didn't like—soon after they came out, and there was a talk about them, he said one day I met him in the Hammersmith omnibus, 'Would you like to have a copy, Miss Macallan?' says he. 'I should, indeed,' says I, quite flattered, though I have rented sittings in the Kensington Free Kirk of Scotland, close by here, these fifteen years, and it was no great return for the outlay, any way. The next morning the book came, and I'm no saying it isn't a handsome book, solid and *soond*, but the day after, when

I had cut half the leaves, came an account,
five and saxpence! What *do* you think of
that?"

"The gentleman ought to have told you it
was not a gift," said May smiling.

"Just so. Wouldn't *you* have thought it
was in a present?"

"Certainly."

Here a loud ring turned the current of Miss
Macallan's thoughts.

"That will be the post. I'm thinking a
letter for you. I don't spend much time
inditing letters."

"I wonder"— began May, knowing that
Madame Falk had not her present address,
when the young rosy-cheeked servant entered
and presented May with a letter from Ogilvie.
She felt her heart beat with sudden pleasure,
but she did her best (and successfully) to keep
an unmoved face.

"It is from Mr. Ogilvie," she said quietly.
"He is so very kind as to send me a few
lines to wish me success in pleasing
you." And she looked up with a pleasant
smile. "He says little more, except that

he hopes to be in London soon, and to call on you, to whom he desires his best regards."

"Oh, indeed. I am much obleeged. Does he say where he is staying?"

"At Marseilles."

"Doesn't he give his address?"

"No. I don't often write. I do not like to trouble him more than I can help."

"Quite right. The post is late. Now, it's my habit to read a portion of Scripture, and ask a blessing on the Word, so it will be quite ten before we are in bed. Will you be so kind as to ring the bell?"

CHAPTER V.

HAVING listened to a portion of Scripture, describing the satisfactory destruction of hostile tribes by the " chosen people," and a prayer to correspond, May wished Miss Macallan good-night, and took an old-fashioned silver candlestick, containing a rather greasy candle, from the hand of Jessie, the dim light of which made darkness barely visible as she ascended the dreary stairs. Her room too looked eerie, and the large four-post bed, the like of which she had never seen before, seemed positively fearsome. It was even a comfort to think Miss Macallan was next door to her, though May reflected that Miss Macallan in a night-cap—and the probability that she wore one was strong—would be an awe-inspiring spectacle.

The room too was curiously bare and bleak, though well furnished in all essentials.

Though the weather was not really cold, the aspect of the dim, desperately clean, apartment struck a chill through her veins, her hands trembled but she could not feel quite dismayed. Having locked her door, and wrapped herself in a warm shawl, she took out her letter to revive herself.

"My dear May," it began, "you were quite right to wait and travel with Mrs. and Miss Conroy; a day or two sooner or later was of no importance to my rather remarkable relative. You must tell me your first impressions of her, when we meet. I trust she makes you comfortable—on this head, you must tell me the truth; send me a line to the club as usual. Do you think Mrs. Conroy will be able to winter in England? I hope to return soon, but the length of my stay in this detestable place depends on the powers that be. Let me warn you that Miss Macallan is cursed with the wildest curiosity respecting everything which does not concern her, so don't let her pump you. I do not suppose she would read your letters, but 'lead her not into temptation,' at any rate burn mine!

"I must stop, for I want this to greet you on your start in life on your own account. May success attend you, and may brighter days soon be yours. When I return I hope to show you something of London. Believe me, my dear ward, to be always your friend,

"PIERS OGILVIE."

This was dated Marseilles. May read it through twice, a half smile of pleasure on her lips. Then she tore it into small pieces and burned them in the candle, throwing the ashes out of the window.

With that variability of temperature to which the inhabitants of this "Isle of Beauty" are accustomed, the "morrow" in May's new abode was dull, with a cold, drizzling rain, and occasional gusts of wind from various points of the compass. The dining-room, when May descended in time for prayers at half-past eight sharp, looked cheerless and depressing, for it was not yet the date at which Miss Macallan permitted

fires to be lighted, but the cardboard folding
screen, on which were depicted roses, dahlias
and chrysanthemums, had been removed from
the cold grate where the coals and wood
were laid, and which looked black indeed.

Miss Macallan had already taken her place
at table, and where her plate ought to have
been a thick, black Bible was placed.

" You'll sit here, please," she said to May,
indicating one of the chairs against the wall.

Jessie, and her young assistant, entering at
the same time, placed themselves as near the
door as they could squeeze, and the lady of
the house proceeded to read a passage from
the Revelations. It was shorter than the
evening portion, so was the prayer, and the
" Amen " was so immediately followed by the
words, " Here, Agatha, infuse the tea as quick
as you can and be sure the water boils ! " that
for half a second May thought it was part of
the petition. Then, having given a pinch of
tea in a large cup to the rosy-cheeked girl,
she turned to her young guest.

" Good morning, Miss Riddell, I hope you
rested well—was your bed comfortable ? "

25*

"It was only too luxurious, Miss Macallan! I had some difficulty in leaving it!"

"Eh! It's not every night you'll sleep in a bed like that! Do you find the room chill? I did not think it worth while setting the fire alight. The sun will be out presently, when the shower has passed, and this room is awful warm in the morning sun."

"Just at present it does not look as if we should ever see the sun again," said May smiling.

"It's a verra changeable climate," returned Miss Macallan seriously, "but if you feel cold, I'll tell Agatha to light the fire."

"Oh, not on my account!" exclaimed May. "Tea will make me quite warm."

"Maybe so! Here's breakfast," as the younger servant brought in a tray.

May was glad to have a cup of hot tea, and Miss Macallan helped her to two of the four scraps of bacon which lay on an elegant silver breakfast-dish.

"The day after to-morrow," resumed Miss Macallan, when she had finished her bacon, and broken some toast into her teacup, "the day after to-morrow I mean to begin fires in the drawing-room; but as it's a year past since the grate was used, I think it is well the vent was seen to first. Then you can use the room every morning and afternoon if you want to play music or anything else."

"You are really too good!" said May, surprised at this consideration. "You must not inconvenience yourself, but if you *can* let me have time to practise I shall be very grateful! I am so glad you have a piano."

"Ah, well, I can't say I have one in the house yet, but my cousin Ogilvie said you would need one, and insisted strongly on my hiring one, so I gave in on that point, but I thought it better you should choose it yourself. There is a verra respectable man lets pianos in the High Street, so if it clears we'll go this afternoon, and you can please yourself."

"Thank you very much, Miss Macallan! Do you like music?"

"Well, yes, I am pleased to hear a Scotch tune, or a hymn, but music never came much

in my way. Anyhow, my cousin Ogilvie
seems to think it right you should have a
pianoforte to play upon and I must keep my
word! Will you take another cup of tea?
No? Then I'll be obleeged to you to ring
the bell. I don't like the breakfast things
longer about than need be—it's just a waste
of time."

May complied.

"I should be very glad, Miss Macallan, if
you would tell me what you wish me to do,"
she said. "I have never been out of my own
home before, and I do not exactly know my
duties."

Miss Macallan's mouth extended itself into
a grim smile.

"You'll not be accustomed to do much,
I'm thinking," she said.

"You are mistaken, I assure you! I have
been in the habit of doing a great many
things, perhaps not very well, but as well as
I could, and I want to be really of use to
you."

"Maybe you'll say what you *can* do?"
asked Miss Macallan dryly.

May laughed and coloured as she returned :

"I can read aloud, and write to dictation, I have done a deal of needlework, and I believe I darn pretty well. I could buy things in France, that is, I know the prices, and I have some idea of arithmetic, not much, for my father was a very good arithmetician, and kept his books, oh, beautifully ! "

" From what I can gather your late father must have been a sensible, far-seeing man," observed Miss Macallan, solemnly.

" He was very clever," returned May, with a far-away look, while she asked herself, " Am I not unnaturally hard not to feel more sorrow for him ? "

"You spoke of darning," resumed Miss Macallan, " I have some napery I set great store by, and they are wearing a bit in the folds, do you feel equal to darning linen ? "

"I think I could, and at all events I shall take great pains."

" Verra well ! I'll give you a tray cloth just to try your hand. I'm fond of needlework myself, but for fine darning my eyes are not just what they were."

"That must be trying," said May. "Knitting is very nice when you cannot see well."

"Ay, I knit a good deal."

"And I could read to you. Perhaps you or your cook would tell me about prices and quantities here, and I might market for you."

"You are a well-disposed girlie," with grave approval. "But I do not think you would be much good at buying, after an up - bringing among careless, extravagant foreigners."

"But, Miss Macallan! if you had lived in France, you would find how wonderfully thrifty French people are. I have heard an English lady, who knew both French and English, say that a French family would live well on what is thrown away in an English kitchen."

"Well! that's something new! Anyway they would not manage to live on what's thrown away in a Scotch one. No, my dear, you must leave the marketing to Jessie and me. I told them at the stationer's by the corner to send me the *Telegraph* every day.

Now I have a young lady to read the paper, I must have a paper to read. Now, come away and I'll show you the house—and I think you'll say it is well kept."

Miss Macallan rose up, seeming to May taller than ever, and, led the way to the topmost attics, into cupboards and closets—especially the linen closet. Every room was well and suitably furnished with the most solid edifices, wardrobes and bedsteads in mahogany and walnut—the beauty and merit of which was duly pointed out—the coverlets of the beds were carefully lifted at the sides to show the cleanliness and high preservation of the mattresses, the curtains were held out to show how well they had been kept from light and dust, though ten, twelve or fifteen years, as the case might be, in use. The drawing-room, which was the grandest part of the show, made May shiver, so utterly was it denuded of all small objects of use or ornament. A large room with three tall narrow windows, innocent of balconies shaded by brocaded stuff curtains (white flowers on a yellow ground) a huge looking-glass set in a

deep gold frame, meandering into illogical
scrolls and curves at the top, more than half
covered the end of the room, and before it,
its natural accompaniment, a marble console
table on which stood a big china vase of
unaccountable shape, the unmistakable ugli-
ness of the Regency period stamped upon it ;
then there were chairs and tables — the
former shrouded in much-washed brown
holland, and strips of looking-glass between
the windows, with another huge one over the
mantelpiece, on which was an ormolu clock,
two more vases and a Dresden shepherd and
shepherdess, a fairly good cabinet inlaid, with
ornamental shelves opposite the windows,
and dwarf book-cases at either side of the
fireplace, filled with the dreariest books,
sermons, theological works, Thompson's
"Seasons," Hume's "History of England,"
and to enliven them, the works of Robert
Burns.

"It's a fine room!" ejaculated Miss
Macallan looking round with pride. "My
late brother worked hard to plenish it, and to
gather the property that kept the house

and "—in a sort of pious, elevated tone—"I
thank the gude Lord that I have been enabled
to keep it well nigh as fresh and sound as he
left it, nigh twelve years. Eh! Andrew, my
man, if you were to walk in this minute, you'd
not find a pin's point changed, and scarce even
reasonable wear and tear. Eh! my word! but
he had a short spell of his grand new house,
my poor brother," and she put her handker-
chief to her eyes.

May was half amused and partly touched
by this curious proof of devotion to a beloved
brother.

"It must have been a terrible loss to you—
his death!" she said softly.

"You may well say so, and it's a large
fortune he would have been master of if the
Lord had spared him," said Miss Macallan as
she pulled down the blinds she had drawn up
that May might see all the glories of the
drawing room. Then she led the way to the
kitchen, the pantry, even the coal cellar, and
everywhere extreme order and cleanliness per-
vaded the premises.

"I haven't gone up and down stairs like

this since the spring cleaning," said Miss Macallan, subsiding into her uneasy "easy-chair," when they returned to the dining-room. "Miss Riddell, my dear! will you bring me my work-bag. It hangs on a nail at the other side of the fireplace—thank you! I am just doing a dozen pair of grey woollen socks for a foolish-like thing they call a 'Christmas Tree.' Our minister is a verra active man, indeed I might say restless, restless as if he had 'a bee in his bonnet,' and he is always devising something to pick the pockets of his congregation —so I do a bit on and off for my contribution, it does not cost so much in the end. Now, suppose you read me a bit of the paper, it's there on the sideboard."

May willingly complied. She was beginning to feel puzzled about her employer. Surely Miss Macallan did not know what she wanted, when she entertained the idea of having a companion. She seemed quite sufficient to herself, to help herself! It would be difficult to discover how one could be of use to such a woman! Existence in her house threatened to be the very lowest, *i.e.*

the least human, form of life May had ever
known or imagined. Still she did not want
to be dismissed, and though Miss Euphemia
Macallan was far from a congenial spirit, she
was at least quite free from the airs of
command, and the dictatorial tone which May
had dreaded, judging by her letter.

For the present, however, she put these
things out of her head, and addressed herself
to read.

" Where shall I begin ? "

" Well—I don't exactly know !   Eh ! just
read over the price list—the stocks and shares,
you know."

" I do *not* know, Miss Macallan, I am sorry
to say ! Whereabouts shall I find it, and
what sort of list is it ?   New Publications ? "

" Gude preserve us !   Where were ye
reared ? I didn't think there was such ignorance in these days. This comes of living
among foreigners ! Give me the paper."

" I am afraid I am very ignorant of many
things."

" Ay ! there it is ! " cried Miss Macallan, after
turning over the paper two or three times,

"I can find it quicker in the *Scotsman*, but there it is sure enough," and she returned it to May. "You just remind me to explain what it all means—some day. It is right down dreadful to leave a young creature ignorant of anything so important as investments! Just you read that, beginning at the beginning."

May dutifully complied and soon stopped at "Egyptian."

"Is it Egyptian Unified?"

"Yes, I think so."

"Well, what's that?"

"The figures opposite are $73\frac{3}{4}$ to 74!"

"Ay! they are going up. Now look for Indian Three per Cents.—but there! give it to me, I ll take my glasses!" cried Miss Macallan. "I'll explain it all to you another time! Just now I cannot be fashed!" She took the paper hastily, and putting her spectacles on her long straight nose, began to skim the prices half aloud with a sort of humming commentary, in an undertone: "Ah! Indian Three per Cents. gone down one-sixteen— that's curious! why should they now?

Consols 98, ex. div. not so bad. Bulgarian, how anyone can risk their money on them! Chilian?—pooh, rubbish! Railway stock. Debenture bonds—no such luck as to have any —Market firm at close. Well, we are not going to smash just yet!"

May listened with some surprise to this unknown tongue, as it was to her.

"Now," said Miss Macallan, returning the paper to her, "you ask me this evening, or some time when I am not much occupied, to explain to you about stocks and shares, and I'll give you a lesson, which I hope you won't soon forget. It's a verra interesting, not to say, important, subject, and I am amazed to think how it came to be omitted from anything that is called education."

" I shall be very pleased if you will take the trouble to complete mine in that direction," returned May, with a smile.

" And that I will"—pleasantly—" I am glad to help a young creature that isn't upsetting and conceited. It's not your fault if your education was neglected; now just look through the paper, and see if there's a remarkable murder, or a divorce case—one must have a little amusement, besides the more important matters."

May searched the columns, but only saw a paragraph in which were the bare fact of an intelligent workman having in an unpremeditated manner kicked his wife to death, and the decision of the judge in the Divorce Court respecting the costs in a cause already tried.

"The paper is rather dull to-day," remarked Miss Macallan, who was knitting energetically, "I canna say it's worth a bawbee."

"There seems to be a very interesting criticism here, on a new play at the Lyceum Theatre; shall I read it?"

"No!" an intensely negative no. "The inside of a play-house I have never seen, and never will! I was brought up by God-fearing parents, that never touched cards, nor looked at play-actors, nor neglected the Sawbbath! and I'm not going to do differently."

"I suppose not!" returned May soothingly, a little startled by this solemn outbreak, "but are there really people now-a-days—I mean, ordinary people——" she hesitated, fearing to

offend, " who think theatres and cards wrong
—that is sinful ? "

" Not many, I am sorry to say! Godliness
and thought for what is lawful and improving,
are fast dying out. I suppose now you have
been often at the play ? "

" Oh, yes ! often."

" Yet you seem a well-disposed, wise-like
girlie ! Did you not feel dazed and, in away,
conscience stricken, when you had been
spending your precious time, looking at a
parcel of bedizened painted jawpies, repeating
lies and nonsense half the night ? "

" Indeed, I did not ! " said May, resisting,
with some difficulty, her inclination to laugh.
" I felt very glad I had enjoyed myself, for I
must confess I love going to the theatre."

Miss Macallan groaned.

" You shall come and hear the Rev. Angus
McCrae on the subject of the devil's devices !
I don't think I'll trouble you for any more of
that paper—I'll just step upstairs and find
you a bit of darning to while away the time
till dinner. Then, if it clears we will go and
see about the pianoforte. I don't want you

to write to my cousin Ogilvie, before it is in
the house. I like to keep my word, and I
want him to know it, so mind you tell him
when you write, and "—with a sudden sharp
look—" when will that be ? "

" Not for two or three days."

" That's right ; men hate to be fashed for
nothing."

This rather wearisome day was a tolerable
sample of many which succeeded it. May felt
that, on the whole, she found favour in her
employer's eyes, and she certainly had a good
deal of time to herself, rather too much for
the satisfaction of her somewhat tender
conscience. She wanted to do more for her
salary, whatever it was to be. This being left
as yet unsettled May supposed, till the end of
her month of trial.

But it was terribly wearisome, this sort of
starved life. Never before had she been
without books, never without intelligent and
even cultivated society. The newspaper and
the piano, and her correspondence with
Frances Conroy and Madame Falk, were her
chief employment and consolation.

Miss Macallan was an untiring pedestrian, and quite out-walked her young companion.

She thought nothing of a march straight to Piccadilly Circus, an hour's perambulation of the Junior Army and Navy Stores, then a ramble up Regent Street, to buy two or three yards of trimming at Peter Robinson's, wherewith to repair a table-cover or a garment (she never seemed to get anything new), then perhaps what she termed "a pennyworth of 'bus" to the Marble Arch, and a walk home across the Park. When she found May too tired to speak after such an expedition, she held forth on the superiority of old-fashioned up-bringing as compared to the "effeeminaency" of modern training!

Still May felt that she was treated with unusual consideration—only—she did not know how long she should be able to endure such a routine.

The last week of October was now on them, and a wild, wet, stormy week it was, playing havoc with the many-tinted leaves in Kensington Gardens, where it was always a treat to May to wander alone.

26*

This particular Thursday, Miss Macallan had gone to the City on some particular business, starting the moment dinner was over, so May, who had reduced her slender and rapidly diminishing store of money, by the purchase of a new song, retired to the drawing-room, intending to have a really good practice.

She was quite absorbed in her occupation, and did not even hear the door open, when she became aware that Jessie was at her elbow, and speaking.

"Here's Mr. Ogilvie himself, and Miss Macallan's no at hame!"

May started up, and saw her guardian on the threshold. Everything seemed absorbed in that delightful sight.

"Oh, how glad I am to see you! I did not dare to hope you would come so soon!" she exclaimed, hastening to meet him with outstretched hands.

He took and held them for a moment, looking into her eyes with an earnest, questioning glance, while his dark face lit up with an expression of pleasure.

"You are quite well, May? 1 need scarcely ask. You look a different creature from—

'The girl I left behind me!'"

and he continued to gaze at her searchingly. Then he looked quickly round the room, at the piano, the fire, a few chrysanthemums in a glass on the table, before he let her go.

"My dear cousin is out, I am told, and will, I hope, stay out. Come May, tell me everything while we are alone together." He said the last words low and softly as if they gave him pleasure.

"Yes, how delighted I am to have such a chance," returned May, a tinge of pink warming her cheek, and deepening the colour in her eyes. "Here, this is a tolerable chair," drawing one near the fire, with a joyous air.

"Am I an old fogey to be taken care of?" asked Ogilvie with his rare sweet smile.

"No! but a good kind friend who ought to be taken care of."

Ogilvie sat down and May took a low child's chair which had made its way by some accident into the sacred room, at the opposite side of the fire. There was a moment's silence.

"Now, my dear ward, begin at the beginning, and tell me everything," asked Ogilvie.

"I have not very much to tell, though it seems such far-away ages since I saw you. Time has gone very slowly," and May proceeded to describe her stay at Audeley Chase, and then the doubt and dread with which she parted with Mrs. Conroy and Frances to dare the terrors of her new life with Miss Macallan.

"Well, and Miss Macallan? you find the house rather ghastly, do you not? Look at me, May!"

"You need not be afraid. I shall tell you the whole truth," she returned with a low happy laugh. "The house was rather wretched after the beauty of Audeley Chase of course. It would have seemed *triste* after our tiny apartment in Paris." She paused and sighed.

"Which you made attractive," murmured Ogilvie.

"But," resumed May, "Miss Macallan was

very kind from the first, and considers me in a way I did not expect. In fact I am more a favoured guest than a companion. I wish I had more to do to earn the salary I suppose I am to get."

"What? Has my estimable relative given you nothing yet? nor opened the subject in any way?"

"No, not yet, but then I have not been here quite three weeks."

"I shall see to that."

"No—no—wait a while; Miss Macallan will soon tell me if I am to stay or not."

"To stay!" he interrupted. "Why yes, of course you will stay!"

"Indeed," continued May thoughtfully, "I often wonder why she ever thought of having a companion. I do not think she wants help in any way, and I do not believe she is inclined to spend more money than she can help. Then she has this piano for my use—but *that* is your doing—" a bright grateful smile and glance—"I think I should have drooped only for it. Why does she want me?"

"You are a close observer, May. However you may depend upon it Euphemia Macallan has her reasons, which probably will remain undiscovered till the crack of doom. She is close-fisted and close-minded, but not altogether bad on the whole—and you get on?"

"Very well indeed. I think she rather likes me."

"I rather think she does. Don't you know May, you are gifted with a curious power of sympathy that makes you quickly indispensable to those who are accustomed to you, especially to the selfish. I am a very selfish fellow, May, and I cannot say how I missed you when we parted. I have been looking forward to seeing you ever since."

"Have you really?" exclaimed May, much delighted.

"Yes, really. If society would permit such an arrangement I should ask you to be my private secretary and we would travel round the world."

"It would be charming!" said May with calm conviction.

"Most charming," echoed Ogilvie, leaning back in his chair and keeping silence for a moment.

"And so you are bored to death?" he resumed.

"That is too strong an expression. It is a very new life to me, but I shall get accustomed to it, and you cannot know, dear Mr. Ogilvie, how grateful I am to you for helping me to escape from the terrible sense of being a burden, a mendicant!" She stretched out her hand and left it in his.

"You are thankful for small mercies, my sweet ward," he said, slowly releasing her hand. "Perhaps some day I may ask some gift which——"

"How glad I should be to be able to do anything for you," she cried, as he paused.

"In the meantime, May, let us make the best of the present. It is a great philosophic achievement to get all the pleasure we can out of life. Would you like to go to the Criterion to-morrow evening?"

"It would be too delicious," clasping her hands.

"Then I shall arrange it with Miss Macallan. I shall stay till she comes in. Now tell me more of our friends the Conroys," and they entered into a discussion of past and present.

Ogilvie told her how he had stopped in Paris to pay a visit to Madame Falk and bring a report of the dear kind woman. Then he mentioned having heard from Madame Zavadoskoï, who was in Russia, whither she had gone to arrange a marriage for her adored son.

The minutes flew fast, and evening was closing in when all too soon the door opened and Miss Macallan in her best "go-to-meeting bonnet" walked in.

"Eh!" she exclaimed in a loud tone. "But this is a most agreeable surprise! And when did you arrive, Cousin Ogilvie?"

"By the mail train this morning," he returned, with a certain air of condescension which struck May. "Lost no time you see in making my ward here give an account of herself. Glad to find that all goes well."

" May be, cousin, you'll stop to take a bit of dinner ? "

"Thank you, no! I am engaged this evening. But I should like to have some talk with you on business, before I go. Good-bye, my dear May! If I can get places for to-morrow night I'll telegraph. Good-bye, glad to see you looking so well." Motioning Miss Macallan to precede him, he paused, and turned to give a parting smile and wave of the hand to his adopted ward.

CHAPTER VI.

"HALCYON DAYS."

MADAME FALK and her partner returned to
their ordinary Parisian life, much invigorated
by their holiday, and further cheered by an
improved offer from an Australian paper, for
which Madame Falk had already written, for
articles treating of political as well as other
gossip. The busy journalist was delighted to
have some more solid subject to deal with,
and set about her fresh work with much spirit
and energy.

Still, both Miss Barton and her cousin felt
the loss of May Riddell very much. There
was always something to interest them in the
pale, quiet girl, who came to them with her
difficulties, her few hopes, her little bits of
success, either in music or in needlework,
humble though they were. It seemed that
with her went everything like progress and

development, and that only the sameness of routine was left.

Her letters were eagerly looked for, especially by Madame Falk, who understood, and was really attached to her.

Miss Barton had a narrower mental range and a less genial temperament, more given to finding flaws than to discovering merit, still May's letters were welcome to her, if only to find fault with them.

Her description of life at Kensington seemed much more terrible to May's friends than she intended it to be ; and Madame Falk greatly rejoiced when she found that Ogilvie had re-appeared and seemed as ever ready to champion his ward.

"He is wonderfully nice and kind," remarked Madame Falk, one raw and uncomfortable evening towards the end of November, as she sat over the fire, having come in from a long ramble, " seeking what she could discover," for her next day's " letter." " Now, at first I thought him cold, haughty, and self-absorbed. It is really hard to judge any one justly, and Mr. Ogilvie had proved me

to be wrong in my conclusions most satis-
factorily," and she folded up May's last epistle
which she had been reading.

"Well, yes. Ogilvie has been very good
to May Riddell," returned Miss Barton, who
had just returned to the *salon* after hanging
up her partner's much-bedrabbled skirt to dry
in the kitchen. "But I fancy it is just a fad.
He pleases himself about it in some way, and
is just as fond of Piers Ogilvie through it all."

"Never mind, Sarah. We have no business
to dig under the surface for motives, let us be
satisfied with the fruit they bear, if it be good
and pleasant."

"'Um, well, perhaps so. There's the bell."

"Yes. I met Mademoiselle Perret this
morning and asked her to dinner."

"You did? Why, Adrienne is out, and the
cloth is not laid."

"What matter? She will be in directly.
Open the door, do, Sarah."

"Ah!" A prolonged "Ah" almost immediately greeted Madame Falk's ears as the
music teacher entered.

"*Bon soir, mesdames.* How truly com-

fortable you look here—the bright fire, the
lamp, the closed curtain. *Dieu!* how cold it
is outside. Dear Mademoiselle Barton, it is
so long since I had the pleasure of seeing you.
Madame I sometimes encounter, always full of
business, always full of energy. Now, the
cold paralyses me. Thanks very much," as
Madame Falk set a comfortable chair for her.
"It is a great pleasure to spend an hour or
two with such kind friends." And the little
woman proceeded to give various details
touching her work. This was her worst
season—strangers had not yet returned to
Paris, regular pupils had not recommenced
their lessons, or had colds—and the firing—
Dieu, it cost dear. It was like burning gold.
Still, she must not complain. On the whole
her "Cours" prospered, and she had the
promise of more pupils after Christmas. So
she talked on till dinner was announced, just
as she had asked, "And that dear child—my
little May?"

"She is quite well. I will read you her
last letter presently," returned Madame Falk
smiling. "Come, Mademoiselle. I hope you

have brought an appetite with you, for we have only a bouillon—*Bifteck au pommes de terre* and *macaroni à l'Italienne*—to offer."

"But it is a repast for an epicure," cried Mademoiselle Perret, joyously, as they sat down.

Having done justice to the *viandes*, the *convives* dallied over their cheese, and Madame Falk read some passages from May's letter.

"Then there is a message for you, Mademoiselle," she continued. "'Tell dear Mademoiselle Perret, with my love, that I am taking singing lessons. My master is an Italian, who is the accompanist to the great Signor V—— and I believe is quite as good a teacher. I think I improve. How I wish I could have an opportunity of having my kind friends' opinion. It is a great pleasure to me to practice, for life here is a little monotonous, though I am ashamed to say this when I am so kindly treated, and so really well off. Mr. Ogilvie is very good in taking me to the theatre, or to a concert when he can, but he has not much time. When he goes away it

will be dull indeed, and, of course, he may go
at any time; but perhaps after Christmas I
may have a holiday, and pay you a little
visit. What joy it would be, especially if I can
pay for my own travels. I spend hardly any
money, and hope to save a good deal of my
salary. I believe you will see Mrs. Conroy and
Frances in Paris soon. Mrs. Conroy caught a
bad cold, and cannot throw it off, they fear
she must go for the winter to Cannes or
Hyères.'"

"Ah, dear, poor lady! It is sad. But I
am charmed to hear so good an account of the
sweet child. I suppose she is well-placed.
The lady she is with is what you call an 'old
maid'?" asked Mademoiselle, who was peeling
an orange.

"Yes; a Scotch lady, and rich; a relation
of Mr. Ogilvie's."

"Then perhaps she will leave our young
friend some of her riches. And Mr. Ogilvie?
I am glad he places her with a relative. He
is an elderly gentleman and unmarried? I
have never seen him—which I regret."

"He isn't young, and he isn't elderly," said

Miss Barton. "He is a cold, silent, well-bred, diplomatic personage, but he was rather intimate with Mr. Riddell, who, it seems, confided his daughter to Ogilvie's care with his last breath, and I am sure nothing short of fearing the judgment that might be coming upon him would have made him give May a a thought."

Mademoiselle shook her head.

"Well, *mes chères dames*, I know your manners and customs are different from ours, but human nature is very much the same in all countries, and it seems to me more or less dangerous that a fascinating man of a certain age should have the care and direction of a charming girl like our dear May."

"I am sure Mr. Ogilvie is by no means fascinating," cried Madame Falk.

"And I am sure I cannot see the remarkable charm of May, though she is a nice good girl!" exclaimed Miss Barton.

"Ah! That is because she hasn't fat, red cheeks, and big white teeth, a figure like an hour-glass, and has not swallowed the poker!" said Mademoiselle with immense fire. "What you English do not understand is grace, softness, thought for others. Then she has eyes —*mon Dieu*, yes, what eyes! Women may not admire her, men will, and this Ogilvie—has he water in his veins or blood? Englishmen may seem cold, frozen, but they have blood in their veins, strong blood, or I mistake much! Then he takes her to the theatre, to the concerts—does the rich Miss go too? No, she is not mentioned! Believe me, it is not wise—it is not safe."

"You certainly do not understand our life nor our habits," replied Madame Falk. "Mr. Ogilvie is a man, I fancy, of great ambition, accustomed to brilliant society, a simple, untrained child like May could only be an object of compassionate kindness—and then he is a man of honour!"

"Honour!" cried Mademoiselle. "Pah! It is inconceivable that a woman of the world, a clever, brilliant woman like you, my good friend, should have the eyes blinded in one direction. There are men everywhere and women are women, silly imaginative beings, who only ask to be allowed to love—anyone.

27*

It is not natural that a clever, worldly man in society should weary himself taking an *ingénue* to see pieces—I suppose fit for an *ingénue* to see, unless there was some motive, some deeper attraction than friendly interest —a guardian's disinterested care for his ward? No, not were he one hundred years of age, and the rich Miss is an imbecile if she believes it. It is possible she may cherish some scheme of marrying them, and settling her fortune upon them. You English are so curiously romantic."

"But supposing your suspicions reasonable, which I do not believe they are, what could we do for May if she were withdrawn from Mr. Ogilvie's protection?"

"Take her yourself! *I* will give her employment, she shall help me with my *cours*, and I will give her twelve francs-fifty a week!" cried Mademoiselle Perret, as if she were promising a fortune; "but take my word for it, May is in a very dangerous position."

"I do not think, Mademoiselle, you at all realise what Englishmen are!" said Miss Barton solemnly.

" I don't suppose they are better or worse than other men," cried Mademoiselle, " but you are all alike, you English ; you say, ' hush, don't say anything shocking,' and shut your eyes, but the ' shocking' happens all the same. If it is nothing worse, the child may break her heart, when he has had enough of his present innocent amusement, and flies off to something new."

" Come, come, Mademoiselle ! This is too much," said Madame Falk. " You excite yourself with your own words. I anticipate no such catastrophe ! Take another orange ? It is barely a month to Christmas, and then she will come and see us, and you will (with your usual acuteness) soon see whether she is as light-hearted as she used to be, though indeed I am not sure she ever *was* light-hearted."

" You are quite too suspicious, Mademoiselle Perret !" added Miss Barton. " It is the fault of most continental people, they are always expecting evil."

" My anxiety has perhaps carried me too far," began Mademoiselle, " but——" she

shook her head sorrowfully, while Miss
Barton sniffed, and Madame Falk seemed
thoughtful.

"Take a little more Bordeaux, dear mademoiselle," she said, rousing herself. "No?
Then call Adrienne, Sarah. If you do not
mind, we will stay here, I fancy the fire in
the *salon* has gone out."

"But certainly! your *salle-à-manger* is all
one could wish."

Gradually conversation on less exciting
subjects was resumed. Mademoiselle Perret
was eloquent about a pupil she had trained
and with whom Monsieur Duval, the fashionable master of the day, to whose class
formerly she had gone for finishing lessons,
had expressed himself highly pleased, a little
talk about dress, a description of the infamous
conduct of the *concierge*, and the little lady,
with a glance at the clock, put up the lace
she was mending, for French women seldom
sit with their hands before them.

"I am keeping you up, dear ladies," she
said, "and I have to rise early myself to-
morrow!" and she proceeded to wrap herself

up. "Oh, I had nearly forgotten to mention that I feel almost sure that I saw your friend, that tall gentleman that used to call here when you hurt your wrist last Spring."

"What, Mr. Carr?" cried Miss Barton.

"His name I never knew, but he was tall and fair, and not quite like other Englishmen."

"Yes, you must mean Mr. Carr. He is an Australian, but I don't think you could have seen him. I rather think he is in Constantinople."

Mademoiselle Perret shook her head.

"I rarely mistake anyone I have once seen," she said. This gentleman came from the 'Hotel Splendide,' and called a *fiacre*, that is all I know. Good-night, dear friends, a thousand thanks for a delightful evening!"

"She is too obstinate and stupid!" exclaimed Miss Barton, when she returned from seeing their guest to the door. "Isn't she?" she insisted, seeing that Madame Falk was in a brown study.

"Yes, I suppose so," returned that lady. "I hope so; one cannot expect a French woman to take the same views we do—I think she is wrong—I—oh, yes, of course, she is!"

"Why, really, Esther, I believe you have grown French yourself! It is past ten, and I am quite sleepy."

"Go to bed then, Sarah. *I* am wide awake, so I will write for a little while. I wish we could afford to have May with us! It is rather cruel to have neither son nor daughter."

"Sometimes it is a good deal more cruel to have them!" said Sarah, with a sniff, as she left the room.

Though Madame Falk wrote far into the night, she was up betimes, as she wished to prepare her Australian letter with care and thought. It was work she enjoyed. It refreshed her after the dry and dusty chronicle of fashion, dress, and Society gossip, and she had done a good morning's work before her partner snmmoned her to breakfast, whereat she was very silent.

"You are meditating some dreadful socialist paragraph, Esther!" said Miss Barton, smiling at her preoccupation.

"No, indeed, nor a radical one either! My editor wants me to put in something about women's rights, and I don't feel at all inclined to handle the subject. I can't make up my mind upon it. I see things cannot go on as they were in our young days, and yet those days were so happy, so delightfully full of pleasant illusions and illogical beliefs, that I should personally prefer going back to them than making the biggest stride forward, but I cannot conscientiously preach such a doctrine."

"Then you must just show up the meanness and cowardliness and unreasonableness of men."

"That I will not. I love them! They have always been good to me. Yes; the generality are not particularly noble, but when they are good, there is no mistake about the goodness, and I can tell you there is nothing in the world so delightful as being taken care of by a kind, generous man."

"You mean it is a delight *I* know nothing about. Well, Esther, I fancy your experience is equally limited."

"Don't be ill-natured, Sarah, let the past rest. *I* can forgive! God only knows where, in my unhappy case, the responsibility of the offender ceased. Anyhow, nature intended men and women to be friends, and it never answers to contradict nature; there, it is a quarter to one. I shall be quite ready by two or half-past, will you be so good as to take my packet to the post? I had such a hard day yesterday that I shall stay indoors to-day."

"Yes, of course; I want to do some shopping, and it is almost dry under foot."

Madame Falk returned to her den, and silence reigned in the apartment for a considerable time, till she issued forth, her papers neatly put up and addressed.

"Please, Sarah, have it weighed. I did not stamp it because—ah! there's the bell! Who can it be? everyone knows my day is Sunday."

"The gentleman who was here in the spring, seeks madame," said Adrienne, entering all in smiles, a card in her hand.

"Why it is Mr. Carr," cried Madame Falk;

"go and speak to him, while I change my dress and put on a top-knot. This old wrap is not fit to be seen!"

After a speedy toilette, Madame Falk went to receive her visitor. She found him walking to and fro the narrow limits of the *salon* as he talked to Miss Barton in his strong cheerful voice. He was looking browner and better-looking than when they had last seen him.

"Ah, Madame Falk," he cried joyously, "I am so glad to see you! I know I have no business to come except on Sunday, but I only arrived last night, and I go off to-morrow morning. So you will forgive the intrusion; I wanted so much to see you."

"I think you are very good to come, and *I* am delighted to see you."

Here Miss Barton took leave and they sat down to talk.

"I fancied you were in Constantinople."

"I was on my way there when I fell in with a very amusing American, who had his yacht at Naples. He took me across to Spain, and then to Marseilles, and there, among the letters forwarded by my bankers, I found one from Conroy asking me to try a few weeks' hunting at Audeley Chase. I thought that was a deuced deal more attractive than Constantinople, so I took the 'rapide' to Paris, and here I am."

After some talk about the Conroys, Madame Zavadoskoi, and other mutual acquaintances, Carr asked:

" Is Miss Riddell still at Audeley Chase?"

" No! she left them at the end of September. She has been rather fortunate in finding an engagement with an elderly lady whose sight is weak or imperfect."

" Ah! and what does she do?"

" She reads aloud—and writes for her, and generally helps her."

"Then I suppose Riddell did not leave much?"

" Not a farthing! That is, his quarter's income (he had sunk all he possessed in a life annuity) had just come in, and when his few debts, his funeral and the mourning were paid, there were about thirty francs left. Mrs. Conroy was as usual most kind and generous, and May had a nice rest at Audeley Chase.

Then there was nothing for her but to go into harness. I can't tell you, Mr. Carr, how terribly we miss her. The place does not seem like home any longer."

" I can imagine it!" cried Carr, rising and taking a turn up and down. "My God! fancy that delicate and refined girl knocking about the world, earning her bread, and a great hulking fellow like me, with his pockets full of money, trying to find out the pleasantest way of spending it!" and he threw himself again into his chair.

" It is a contrast I grant! But, believe me, there is something exhilarating in winning one's own bread, if you are so lucky as to get the chance of winning it! I think May is rather fortunate; she is evidently treated with kindness and consideration. You see, this lady with whom she lives—Miss Macallan—is a relation of Mr. Ogilvie's, who placed her there—you remember Mr. Ogilvie here last spring?"

"Ogilvie placed her there?" in a tone of great surprise. " Why, what the——I mean what had *he* to do with it?"

" Why, Mr. Carr, did I not tell you, when I wrote, that Mr. Ogilvie was with Mr. Riddell when he met with his fatal accident? It seems that the last words Mr. Riddell spoke were to ask Ogilvie to take care of May."

" He asked Ogilvie ! why — had he no relations—or——It seems strange to me——"

"I must say Mr. Ogilvie has been most kind and helpful. I never expected he could have been so nice. I don't know what we should have done without him. You see, as an employé of the British Government and connected with the Embassy, he could do more than anyone else with the tiresome French officials. Then he went off to Scotland and somewhere else, but he managed to secure this Miss Macallan for May, who really is as happy with her as she could be with any one, except perhaps, myself," she added with her bright kindly smile. " Pray admire 'my conceit."

" It is not conceit, it's the truth, Madame Falk !" said Carr gravely. "I wish you would give me Miss Riddell's address. I suppose I might call and see her? I should like to do so."

"Of course you may! I will write it for you; but if you call I should like to send her a little present, by you."

"So you can! I am at the Hotel Spendide, and will take anything you like!"

"My parcel will not be much—only a few pairs of gloves."

"Very good! but I am obliged to go straight through to Kingsford, for Mr. Conroy tells me he must escort his wife and daughter to the Riviera before Christmas, so I promised to be with him on Saturday. But I intend to stay a while in London afterwards, and then I shall have the pleasure of handing your parcel to Miss Riddell. Now pray write me the address—while you think of it."

Madame Falk complied, and Carr put the morsel of paper on which it was written in his note-book.

"And are you going back to Australia in the spring?"

"I rather think not. There is so much to see in these grand old countries. My plans

are all unsettled. In short, I have thrown
the reins on the neck of the future, and will
go where it takes me."

A little more talk about Madame Falk's
new line of work, a little argument (as was
usual between them) respecting politics and
principles, and Carr took his departure.

"That's a capital woman," was his reflection, as he descended the stairs. "For
though she does man's work, she is every
inch a woman."

"He is an honest young fellow!" mused
Madame Falk. "But already corrupted by
riches. He would keep down the working
man, and he cannot see the educational value
of political rights."

*   *   *   *   *

In London the weeks had flown with
wondrous speed for May Riddell since
Ogilvie's appearance on the scene. He
generally spent the greater part of Sunday
with his relative in Granby Road. That is,
he came to luncheon and, if fine, took May
on some expedition by road or rail; if wet,
to some church to hear either fine music or

fine preaching — no matter if Protestant,
Catholic, or any other of the seven hundred
and fourteen denominations said to be
registered within the borders of the great
city. But the crowning benefit bestowed
by this most considerate guardian was the
instruction in music which he insisted on
procuring for her.

At first with blushes and hesitation, yet
with some persistence, she urged that she had
no right to accept so costly a benefit from
him. He however was still more persistent.
He urged that the teacher he selected, though
capable, was as yet unknown and therefore
moderate in his charges, that he was a young
man in whom he (Ogilvie) took an interest
and was anxious to serve, so in engaging him
to teach his ward, he was doing a service to
both for the same cost. May therefore gave
in, as she always did, and greatly profited by
the instruction.

The only person not completely satisfied by
the arrangement was Miss Macallan herself.

Ogilvie had in a private interview insisted
on his cousin being present at the lessons.

" What's the good ? " she asked.

" I do not suppose there is any real necessity," he returned in a hard, commanding tone—very different from the voice to which May was accustomed. " But considering the views entertained by society, it is right that Miss Riddell should have a chaperon present—at all events, I desire it."

This form of expression was generally used by Ogilvie when he wished to clinch an argument with Miss Macallan, and he had never found it to fail.

" It's not just the pleasantest way to pass an hour, that ought to be between lights ; instead of resting one's eyes with forty winks, to be blinking in that big drawing-room, with the two candles on the piano, listening to all that skirling up and down," was her confidential remark to her prime minister.

" Ah, Jessie, my woman. She's a nice douce girlie, but nothing so verra remarkable. Mark my words, she has a big fortune waiting her somewhere, and my kinsman knows all about it ; he's a cunning chiel, and small blame to him."

" May be so, mem, an' I'm sure if the young leddy has thousands and thousands she might be proud to tak' him. He is a grand gentleman, but to my thinking more like a father than a lover."

" Hoot-toot, Jessie. What do you know about it ? "

" Weel, mem, it's just what every woman high and low *does* ken."

" Anyhow I'm getting on fine with my socks for the Kirk Christmas sale, and Miss Riddell is doing a shawl just beautiful." Thus Miss Macallan.

Ogilvie, with the fatherly interest perceived by the lynx-eyed Jessie, was careful to acquaint himself with the progress made by his ward. And often came of an evening after his dinner (for the Granby Road *cuisine* did not exactly suit him) to hear May sing. On these occasions Miss Macallan naturally spared herself the additional " skirling," coming in for a few minutes to ask if the coffee which May had taught Jessie to make was to her kinsman's " liking." " There's no use in me staying to listen to all the havers

28*

they talk," she said to herself " about books and pictures and out-o'-the-way things, not a word of sound doctrine amongst it all."

Her absence was not ˙much noticed by either of the interlocutors as they rambled from subject to subject between May's songs, nor was she averse to hold her own in opposition to her guide, philosopher and friend.

She was too frank, too honest, to be afraid of making mistakes or seeming foolish ; so from these discussions she received a greater amount of education than she was aware. Then the books he lent her were interesting and awakening. Altogether it was a heavenly time for May, sprinkled as it was with occasional visits to the best theatres and, when the weather permitted, expeditions to places worth seeing in the neighbourhood of the town.

" You are really making progress, May," said Ogilvie one evening some little time after the date of Carr's visit to Madame Falk, when he had asked for one song after another. " I don't mean to say you will ever be anything remarkable, but you sing in perfect tune, which is rare, and you have expression; you might have more, if you would let yourself go. I fancy there are possibilities of passion under the soft-snow of your exterior!"

"That I do not know—but I hope I may learn Signor G——'s method—it is very like Mademoiselle Perret's—I might then be able to teach, which would be a great help to me, for I cannot expect Miss Macallan to keep me always."

"Nor, I imagine, would you like to stay," observed Ogilvie.

"Yes, I should, so long as you are in London and able to come and see me; otherwise—well, I should like to go back to Paris."

"So you find me not a bad sort of chum?" he returned, resting his elbow on the table, and shading his eyes with his hand.

"I do not think there is any one else quite like you—at least, I never met anyone the least like you. But, of course, you cannot be here always—nor can you come always so often."

"No, unfortunately; the private secretary-ship would be the thing, eh, May?"

"Ah, yes. I wish it could be."

There was a pause during which May knitted diligently.

Then she ventured to say: "I heard a lady, Mrs. Montgomery, at Audeley Chase say that you might go to Japan."

"Did she? How the deuce did she hear that? Well, there was some talk of it, but I do not want to go. In fact, I have perambulated the earth long enough. I want to stay in England, and if possible have a finger in the management of this tight little island."

"I should like to hear you speak in the House of Commons," said May.

"You would be exceedingly disappointed then, I have no gift of eloquence. There are some obstacles, however; I am not rich enough for free action."

"I thought you were well off, if not very rich."

Ogilvie laughed. "I am considerably better off than I was, my sweet friend," he said. " I have quite enough to jog along comfortably, but I am not quite satisfied with that sort of life. You see, I confide in you, though you are rather young to be the recipient of confidence from a battered worldling like myself."

" Your heart is kind and fresh still," said May quietly.

" It is a good deal fresher than I imagined," murmured Ogilvie as if to himself.

" At all events," May went on, "you may be sure I will never repeat a word you say."

" No, I do not suppose you will—but I want you to promise more. I want you never to mention me, in your conversation or your letters, to Frances Conroy, or to Madame Falk, or anyone."

" Very well—I promise—but, Mr. Ogilvie, I have often mentioned you to Madame Falk. I told her how kind you were—how you had given me music lessons, and many other things."

" Ah ! Then pray be satisfied with the eulogiums you have already penned, and do not mention me any more; let me rest in the shade like a beautiful flower."

"Very well," said May with a smile. "I shall remember."

There was another pause, during which Ogilvie watched May's fingers, which swiftly yet quietly plied the needles.

"I met Madame Laldeschi when I was at Marseilles, and we had quite a long talk."

"Madame Laldeschi?" repeated May. "I don't think I know her."

"You have seen her. Do you remember a tall lady in grey at the Zavadoskoï ball?"

"Yes, a lady with a charming sad face. I remember her quite well, you said you respected her!"

"That is Madame von Nierhoff. She is a charming good woman. She was taking one of poor Laldeschi's daughters, a very delicate girl, to Nice for the winter. The mother was kept in Paris by business"

"You said she was their dear friend."

"She was their providence, but she had been Laldeschi's great friend originally, she was his most faithful confidant and assistant, all through the Italian troubles. Then, being poor, considering his rank, he was obliged to marry the countess for her fortune; he was a very good husband, I believe, and his wife is greatly attached to Madame von Nierhoff."

"I do not think if I had been his wife," began May, "I should have liked——"

Her further speech was interrupted by the entrance of Miss Macallan.

"Good evening, Cousin Ogilvie, I could not come in before. The minister of our kirk just stepped in to ask my opinion respecting the children's treat at Christmas-time, and as suchlike things are not exactly in your line, I stayed to hear him. How was the coffee?——" and the privacy of the evening was over.

CHAPTER VII.

"A LITTLE CLOUD."

FRANCES CONROY was not a satisfactory correspondent—sometimes she wrote a couple of letters in quick succession, and then weeks would go by before she broke silence; May always wrote at regular intervals, and told her friend of the routine of her simple life, but even before Ogilvie had warned her she was instinctively cautious in mentioning him, as he had perhaps unconsciously impresssed her with the idea that he hated being gossipped about.

She was grieved to find that Mrs. Conroy had taken cold, and though they had found a pretty villa, and the invalid wished very much to remain through the winter near her friends, she was imperatively ordered abroad.

May, therefore, expected them to pass through London, and looked every morning for a letter, telling her where to call and

enjoy a talk with her good friends, before
they departed for some southern health resort.

Three or four days passed, however, and
none came, nor had Ogilvie paid his usual
evening visit.

On the Monday following the conversation
detailed in the last chapter, a note from him
awaited her on the breakfast-table.

It was dated the previous Saturday, and
bore the address " Rockborough Castle, near
Greystone, Yorkshire."

" DEAR MAY,

" I have been called suddenly from Town,
but shall return before Saturday next. Should
you want anything, a letter to this address
will find me. I hope you practise diligently
and will make great strides in my absence.

" Always yours,
" P. OGILVIE."

Then it would be a whole week before she
should see him. How intolerably long the
time would seem!

She told Miss Macallan, who said:

"Rockborough Castle—that is some grand place! Let me see, I have a fine book about the country seats of the nobility and gentry, my poor dear brother used to read in it, and make long calculations about the value of these pleasure-places being lost to the nation. He was wonderful strong in figures! Agatha!" to the younger servant, who was adding water to the tea-pot, " go into the back-parlour, and bring me a big brown and gold book, that lies on the little table in the window."

The girl obeyed.

Miss Macallan put on her spectacles, opened the huge volume, and drew her finger down the index.

"Ay, here it is: 'Rockborough Castle, Yorkshire, the seat of the Right Honourable the Earl of Shelbourne.' Yes, Cousin Ogilvie knows a grand lot of fine people."

"Shelbourne," repeated May, "I have seen that name in the paper, I am sure."

"He is one of the Ministers, I am thinking," observed Miss Macallan, and she went on with her breakfast.

As soon as the cloth was removed, May proceeded to perform almost the only duty demanded by her employer, which was to read the newspaper.

Glancing through it to find the horrors, that always interested her hearer, her eye caught a morsel of fashionable intelligence.

" The Secretary for Foreign Affairs, who has been suffering from severe bronchial cold, remains at Rockborough Castle for a few days longer, and has benefited by the change of air."

" Lord Shelbourne is the Foreign Secretary," she said, and read aloud the paragraph.

" Ah ! just so," remarked Miss Macallan. " He'll be sent as ambassador somewhere one of these days himself, you'll see—I mean my Cousin Ogilvie."

" Very likely indeed," thought May, and through all her reading aloud, a sort of melancholy refrain sounded in her heart. " He will be sent somewhere far away, and these pleasant days will pass, never to return."

" Are you quite yourself this morning, my dear ? You are just reading as if you didn't understand the words before you?" asked Miss Macallan, looking up from her thirty-fourth sock.

"Thank you, I am quite well, only a little more stupid than usual."

"Well, you needn't read any more now. I am going downstairs to Jessie; she is making a Christmas bun to-day, and would you please write for two tons of coal—mind you say ready money, so they must put the net price on the bill, and there's the grocery order for the Civil Service Stores, after that you may go skirl to your heart's content."

"Thank you"—laughing—"I shall put off my skirling till after dinner. I want to write to Madame Falk, I have not heard from her for such a long time."

Miss Macallan left the room, and May sat down to her writing—she did not get on rapidly, however. The idea of losing Ogilvie's society, his care, his encouragement, was positively appalling. The delight of being valuable to him as a friend, almost a confidant,

was infinitely flattering, infinitely sweet. It
raised her in her own estimation. He was
the only creature who seemed to recognise
what she felt to be true, that she had some
sense, some taste, some perception. Madame
Falk, kind and sympathetic as she was, treated
her as a good, gentle, and rather unhappy
child, as if she were still what she had been
six years ago, for she was too busy to be able
to observe much, but Ogilvie looked upon her
as a friend, almost an equal. He who was so
experienced, so intellectual, so in every way
superior, how was she to bear her everyday,
common-place life if she were never to see
him? To this question she sought in vain for
an answer.

"There's a gentleman seeking you!" exclaimed Jessie, offering May a card, and
looking very cross at being called away from
her cooking because Agatha was upstairs.

"Mr. Carr!" cried May, starting up, and
going towards the door to meet him as he
entered; "how very glad I am to meet you,
and how good you are to come all this
way!"

Carr's face lit up with a pleasant, gratified smile at her cordial greeting.

" Good to myself," he said. " I only came up to Town last night from Audeley Chase, and I must apologise for this early visit, but I have various engagements in the afternoon, and early to-morrow I go out of Town for a few days; you will excuse me? "

" Indeed I do! It seems as if dear Madame Falk must be coming, too, you are so associated with her in my mind. Did you see her before you left. She mentioned that you were going to the Chase, but that was some little time ago."

" Yes; I paid her a long visit, she seemed as well and as bright as ever—misses you awfully, she says. Indeed, the place does not look itself without you. Madame Falk is very anxious to know how you are, and if you are comfortable."

" If you see her again you must set her mind at rest on that score. Few girls who are companions are so kindly treated and so free as I am." She stopped abruptly, for she could hardly stop the words, " and we see Mr. Ogilvie very often," which were on the very tip of her tongue when the recollection of his dislike to being gossiped about arrested them.

"I must say," considering her with grave attention, "that you are looking uncommonly well. But, somehow, you are changed, you seem less shy, less cold, and older; excuse my free speech, you know I always felt at home with you."

"How can you expect me to forgive you for saying I look older?" returned May, with a grave, sweet smile, which struck Carr as very charming.

"Yes, I do. You would, if I could express *how* you seem older. I am always rather an inarticulate sort of fellow."

"Are you? *I* have not found you inarticulate. Now, tell me, how is Miss Barton?"

"I only saw her for a few moments. She is the same as ever. Just as porcupiny! Perhaps I ought not to say so to you."

"Perhaps not. But I understand. Believe me, there is a heart under the quills. I used to think she did not like me; indeed, I do not think she likes anyone except her cousin. But in my time of need she was wonderfully kind to me. How I should like to go back to them, only——"

"Then, why don't you?" interrupted Carr eagerly. "I'll escort you. I've nothing to keep me anywhere, or take me anywhere. You and I are not conventional. This seems a dull hole. You must be moped to death."

"I am not, indeed. Then, you see, I have an employment here; it is by no means sure I should find any in Paris."

"You are wonderfully plucky," admiringly.

"I am afraid I cannot accept that praise. My way has been wonderfully smoothed for me."

"I suppose you see Ogilvie sometimes?" asked Carr, looking keenly at her.

"Oh, yes. He is exceedingly good in caring for me. Miss Macallan, the lady of the house, is his cousin. She is wonderfully Scotch, and very considerate to me."

"And what do you do all day? I must be prepared at all points for Madame Falk's questions."

May gave him a short sketch of her life in Granby Road, including her singing lessons.

"I did not know you sang!" he exclaimed. "I should like to hear you."

"Mine is a very feeble kind of singing. Mr. Ogilvie thinks that, although I shall never do much, if I understand how to sing I can teach, which will be very useful for me."

"Oh, that's what Ogilvie thinks, is it!" Then with an abrupt change. "I am afraid Mrs. Conroy is very delicate. There was a letter from the daughter yesterday, and Mr. Conroy started off at once to make arrangements about her journey to the Riviera, that is the reason I left."

"Dear Mrs. Conroy," began May, when the door opened, and Miss Macallan appeared in her best shot silk, and afternoon cap, her curls freshly and stiffly rolled at either side of her face, and black lace mittens on her bony hands.

Carr rose and made his best bow.

"This gentleman is a friend of Mrs. Conroy's," said May, "whom I used to know in Paris. Mr. Carr—Miss Macallan."

29*

" Oh, indeed! I'm pleased to see you, sir ; pray, sit down."

Carr obeyed. An awful pause ensued.

" The weather is verra changeable," re-marked Miss Macallan, at last.

" Well, yes ; but not as bad as I expected. I never was in England at this time of the year before."

" But you are not a Frenchman, I am thinking ? "

" No. I came from Australia."

" Eh, but that's a long way. I suppose you have come to settle in England, though you look rather young to have made your fortune ? "

" Thank you," he returned, smiling. " I hope to return to my Australian home as soon as I have seen a little more of Europe. I have promised to see Miss Riddell, and take a report of her to some very particular friends of hers in Paris. I must say you seem to have taken excellent care of Miss Riddell. I never saw her look so well. But I confess I had a sort of commission to steal her away from you if I could. Her old friend Madame Falk is very anxious to have Miss Riddell with her for a short time, if you can spare her."

"Well, she'll no have her!" interrupted Miss Macallan. "Why she hasn't been in my house three months yet, and her guardian placed her under my care, so here she must stay."

"Is Ogilvie really your guardian?" asked Carr.

"He is so good as to consider himself my guardian," said May. "But I have no right whatever to expect a guardian's care from him."

"Just so!" chimed in Miss Macallan. "It is not every girlie that has a man like him—a fine, rising man, that will be an ambassador one of these days—to look after her and think of every little thing, and come out of an evening, wet or dry, after the work of the day, to hear her sing, and see if she's profiting by the instruction he is giving her. She cannot be grateful enough, *I* tell her."

"I *am* very grateful," said May quietly.

"Yes. It is quite remarkable," ejaculated Carr.

"Yes, that's just what it is," said Miss Macallan, emphatically.

"Well, Miss Riddell," said Carr rising, "I have overstayed the limits of a merely polite visit. When I return next week may I call again? I have stupidly forgotten a parcel Madame Falk entrusted to me. I shall certainly bring it next time."

"Ah, yes! pray come. I shall be so pleased, and I shall have a little packet for my dear, good friends, if you will take it for me. Pray, let me have a post-card, that I may be at home."

"Thank you very much. I shall not fail to let you know. Good-bye, Miss Riddell; good bye, Miss Macallan."

He left the room, followed by May, who never thought of ringing the bell in the proper style. She therefore exchanged another good-bye, which Carr supplemented with a whispered "She looks awfully grim."

"Weel," said Miss Macallan, who was more than ever convinced that May had a big fortune awaiting her somewhere, "I don't know much about the ways of the world as it is now, but I don't think it is quite the thing for a young leddy to go out to the door alone, to say a last good-bye to a young man, and a verra good-looking young man."

"But, Miss Macallan, am I not to show him civility because he happens to be nice?" asking May laughing.

"That is not just the right kind of answer to give me," said Miss Macallan sternly. "Moreover, I minded that you told the young man you would stay at home if he wrote you, which is not exactly the reserve of a modest maiden. I am no that sure your guardian, Mr. Ogilvie, would quite approve!"

"I am sure he would not disapprove," said May, surprised and amused, yet a little nettled. "My guardian knows Mr. Carr very well. He knows, too, that Mr. Carr used to be often at the Conroys' and Madame Falk's; dear Miss Macallan, there is nothing wrong or remarkable in Mr. Carr writing to say he will come and see me! It is quite funny that you should think so," and she laughed in a frank, amused way that made Miss Macallan see that she was rather making a mountain of a mole-hill.

"Varra weel!" she said deliberately. "Young women are not what they used to be, and I suppose I do not know the difference between right and wrong — any way, I hope you'll tell Mr. Ogilvie of this visit."

"Yes, of course, I shall!" cried May. "It will be something to talk about when he comes back."

"I can't say you seem to have any lack of things to talk about," returned Miss Macallan dryly; and feeling somehow that she had not scored in this slight passage of arms, she betook herself to the kitchen, and covering her gorgeous shot silk with a cook's apron, she lent a scientific hand to the preparation of a very elaborate Christmas bun.

May was greatly pleased to see Carr again. He was associated in her mind with the first few happy days she had known since she awoke (and how soon she was awakened) to the fact that she had neither value nor importance in her father's eyes, that she was in truth a profitless, costly burden, though in public he always treated her with caressing politeness.

Then Madame Falk's compassionate kindness had been the first balm poured into her wounds, and the deep sense of gratitude called forth by that good woman still burned as warmly in her heart as the first moment that Madame Falk's hearty kiss had set it alight in her chilled, starved heart.

But it was only last spring that the delicious conviction had grown upon her that other people began to find her neither dull nor insignificant.

Carr had always been friendly and ready to talk to her, or dance with her, and how delightfully he danced! She had deeply enjoyed that ball at the Zavadoskoï Hotel.

It was there, too, that Ogilvie first began to treat her as if she were somehow different from others, as if she were a creature he could speak to on equal terms. It seemed to her that she had never really lived before that period of emancipation.

Yes, she was indeed very glad to see
Carr, yet it disturbed her to have all these
memories so suddenly evoked, and now was this
short space of brightness to be clouded over
by the "blackness of darkness?" If Ogilvie
was to be despatched to the other side of the
world, what was to become of her? She did
not feel able to answer that terrible question
within the narrow limits of the house, and
leaving word that she had gone to walk in
Kensington Gardens, as she had a slight
headache, May wrapped herself up and was
soon in the open air.

No, it would be impossible, she acknow-
ledged to herself, to go on living with Miss
Macallan. There was an indescribable
sordidness about life in Granby Road, and
absence of everything approaching interest,
yet what could she do?—here, at least, her
material wants were provided for; could she
be sure of earning sufficient for that purpose
if she went to Paris? For if she lost Ogilvie,
her only refuge would be with Madame Falk,
and she had no right to bueden that generous
woman more than she was already burdened.

Perhaps her guardian, as she generally called
him in her mental discussions, had some
such idea in his head, when he insisted on her
taking singing lessons. As this thought
presented itself to her mind a shiver ran
through her. It flashed across her how
utterly her whole being had entwined itself
round him. Was it not appalling to find that
the possibility of happiness or wretchedness
hung on so mere a thread as the chance of
his being kept in London or sent abroad, for
if it were merely across the Channel it would
effectually be separation. Then she saw that
this grave, calm guardian was all the world
to her—that she loved him with all the force
of her deep tender heart. She did not shrink
from the discovery. Why should she not love
him? True, he was not likely to give her
such affection as filled her soul; he was not
a character to have such a feeling or develop
it, but as long as he gave her the considerate
friendship, the delicious sympathy he had
already so abundantly bestowed, that was
enough—quite enough. Her own love for
him would be a sweet secret between herself

and her heart. None need ever know it—
Ogilvie least of all. He did not want
marriage or domestic ties. What he wanted
was an utterly devoted friend whose ear was
ever ready to hear, and whose understanding
was not unequal to comprehend his difficulties,
his aims,—to whom he could speak as to a
second self and whose whole soul was his, as
no man friend's could be. Was this not a
noble task for any woman? It seemed completely satisfying to May, only she prayed not
to be parted from him. What news would he
bring back with him from this visit to the
Foreign Minister? She did not at all dread
meeting him. She had no fear of betraying
herself, his calmness would keep her composed. Indeed, though strong and profound,
she felt that her love was like a deep, abounding river, the surface of which was so smooth
and unbroken from its own fulness that none
might guess the force of the current.

This long commune with self seemed to
revive her courage. Something seemed to
tell her that Ogilvie would not leave England,
at all events, he would return on Saturday,

and on Sunday she should certainly see him; that thought was enough to send golden edges to the dark cloud lowering over her at present, and she returned much more hopeful and at the same time resigned to confront the reproachful looks of Miss Macallan, for May was ten minutes late for dinner.

" I am so sorry! " she exclaimed apologetically. " I had no idea how the time was going."

" Haven't you a watch ? "

" Yes, but I seldom wear it."

" More's the pity! It's just a mercy we have Scotch broth for dinner, and they can stand any amount of cooking. Do you have a lesson this afternoon ? "

" Yes, Miss Macallan, instead of to-morrow. Signor G—— has been a little irregular lately."

" You light the fire in the drawing-room, then," to the girl who was waiting, "and don't unroll the hearth-rug till it's well lit."

" I will attend to the fire; I am going to practise before my lesson."

" The walk has given you a bit of colour in your cheeks," said Miss Macallan, looking at her. " It's a pity you cannot keep it there, for it makes almost a bonny lass of you."

" Whereas in my true colours, which are rather pallid, I am anything but ' bonnie,' " said May good-humouredly.

" I will not say that exactly," returned Miss Macallan, " but after all, handsome is, that handsome does."

" Yes, that is the best sort of beauty," said May, as she left the room to attend to the drawing-room fire, and prepare for her lesson.

*   *   *   *   *

The rest of the week went fast enough. May could always find occupation; besides, the weather was fine, crisp and bright, permitting of out-door exercise.

Ogilvie did not write, and May, always careful not to trouble him with unnecessary letters, sent no reply to his, as it did not seem to want one. Saturday came at last. The previous evening came a note from Carr.

" I shall have the pleasure of calling to-morrow afternoon—should you be engaged, pray mention when I may find you."

May did not feel it necessary to communicate this note to Miss Macallan.

That lady was going out, though not to shop. For a wonder she had been invited to luncheon with a Scotch family with whom at long intervals she had exchanged visits for some years, and who resided at Hampstead.

It was therefore a serious undertaking. She had her breakfast half an hour earlier than usual. She made elaborate provision for the needs of the ensuing Sabbath, and left a whole string of directions with the faithful Jessie. In short, it wanted but a quarter to twelve when she got under weigh.

May, with her ready politeness, put on her hat and cloak to escort her to the omnibus, and took the opportunity to buy a few flowers on her homeward way, in order to beautify the drawing-room, and so assist in presenting her present abode in the most favourable light. Then she put on her best dress—her second-best was getting a bit worn—but, thank Heaven! she would be able to replace it after Christmas. How delightful it was to earn money, though she certainly would be glad to do a little more for her employer. She could not be quite worth what she cost, and it puzzled her to account for Miss Macallan's willingness to maintain an unnecessary mouth. It was a contradiction to all her other characteristics. " Nor does she care much for me," thought May, " though she is nice and civil enough. Indeed, I am ashamed to find that I would not be grieved to part with her for ever." So thinking she sat down to the piano, and began to play some of the airs she had picked up by ear. She had placed the piano across a corner from whence the door could be seen.

She had not been dreaming over her music long when Carr arrived, armed with Madame Falk's parcel—a delightful quantity of hot-house flowers, loose, and pinned up in white paper. May was charmed and grateful; she demanded water and a tray at once, and set about filling what bowls and vases she could find with deft fingers.

Carr sat watching her, highly pleased. He found his silent, quiet friend of the Rue Vielle Cour greatly changed, and yet the same in her gentle movements, in her readiness to listen rather than to speak, and a certain reposeful harmony expressed both in face and figure. Against these old traits were to be balanced greater freedom and fluency of speech and increased warmth and frankness of manner. Her cordial and unaffected reception of himself pleased him immensely. Carr was really fond of women. He liked their society, he believed in them, but he was not given to fall in love indiscriminately.

Madame Zavadoskoï had roused a degree of fiery admiration, in which there was little or no esteem, but of sentimental love he had known little or nothing. Now he watched May moving to and fro, and arranging her flowers with a delicious sense of being soothed, of being thoroughly at home. She was fairer than she used to be. Always pale, there was now the faintest tinge of colour in her face, a greater depth of blue or grey, or hazel, he could not tell which, in her eyes, but he was

quite sure about the expression, the sort
of sad, questioning look which was
habitual, but now often varied by a smiling
or serious glance, as if she gave you her
earnest attention. Her figure was still slim,
but not so thin as it used to be, while her very
simple dress, drawn in folds from the shoulder
to the waist, seemed to him wonderfully
graceful, and her throat looked snowy white
as it rose above the black crape frill that
finished her corsage. As he gazed at her
admiringly they talked easily of their Parisian
memories ; and Carr gave her the latest news
of Mrs. Conroy—she was a little better, but
her husband was anxious to hasten her departure to a milder climate. They would
probably pass through town next week.

"And are you really happy here?" said
Carr, after a pause.

"I am, indeed. Why do you ask?"

"Because that Miss What-do-ye-call-em
looks as if she was made of stone, flint! I
cannot fancy your being happy with her."

"I assure you she is very nice to me, I
have nothing to complain of."

" It must be perfectly awful living the same round day after day ; you would be ever so much better off in Paris."

May shook her head.

" I must stay where I am for the present. I have a good deal to interest me. I like my singing lessons."

" Ah, by the way ! Do let me hear you sing. I remember your singing with Miss Conroy, ages ago—that is, last spring, and I thought you had a very sweet voice. Do sing me a song; I love music—in a rude uncultivated manner."

" If you care to hear, I shall be happy to sing for you, but I have but little voice, and Mr. Ogilvie says I shall never do much with it."

" Does he? Oh, well you know, he is a hypercritical, snuff-the-moon sort of fellow. I am much more easily pleased."

May sat down and sang a simple ballad, sweetly and tenderly. At the end of the first verse Carr came over from his seat by the fire, and leant on the piano, charmed and touched by the pathos of her voice. The

30*

song was not yet quite finished, when the door opened and Ogilvie entered unannounced and paused on the threshold contemplating the tableau before him with a look in his eyes and on his brow and mouth, such as May had never seen there before, a look that sent a shiver of painful anticipation through her veins. It was gone in a second and replaced by an expression of icy composure as he advanced into the room.

"Mr. Ogilvie," exclaimed May, rising to meet him and growing very white, Carr observed: "I did not expect you would return so soon."

" Yes, I am a little sooner than I expected," he said, just touching the hand she offered.

" Mr. Carr! I had no idea you were in Town, I heard you were at the Conroys ; hope you had good sport there."

Carr replied, and a somewhat constrained conversation ensued—some sudden paralysing cloud seemed to have fallen upon them, some sinister influence seemed to emanate from Ogilvie, who spoke formally on various ordinary topics, enquired for Madame Falk, and only once addressed May, when he asked if Miss Macallan was at home.

Carr endeavoured in vain to be bright and cordial, but some spell had fallen upon him.

" Where are you putting up ? " said Ogilvie to Carr, after a short pause.

" At the ' Grand,' it is very central and convenient."

" Do you make any stay ? "

" No, not now, I shall run over to Paris next week, and," turning to May, " you spoke of having a parcel or package for Madame Falk. May I call for it on Monday or Tuesday ? "

" Miss Riddell will forward it to you on Monday. It is quite unnecessary to bring you all this way when your engagements are no doubt numerous. The parcel shall be sent," said Ogilvie, in tones so harsh and decided that the sentence sounded like forbidding him the hou·e.

" I can perfectly well come here for it— if Miss Riddell will permit me," began Carr quickly.

" Thank you very much," interrupted May,

" but as Mr. Ogilvie says, I can send it quite well."

" Oh, by all means," returned Carr, in a rather peculiar tone, " but when I come back to London after Christmas, I shall certainly pay you a visit and bring you the latest news. Madame Falk will be delighted to have my report, and for the present I must say good-bye."

" Good-bye! and thank you very much for coming to see me," said May.

" Yes, it was quite a friendly act," added Ogilvie, with an unpleasant smile, and he followed the visitor downstairs with ceremonious politeness, and May remained standing by the fire, a curious dread of coming unpleasantness pressing on her spirit, instead of its being buoyant with the joy, the exhilaration of Ogilvie's return.

CHAPTER VIII.

WHEN Ogilvie returned, he walked straight to
the fireplace, and stood at the side farthest
from May, gazing at the flames for a full
minute—and May, feeling unaccountably
nervous, could wait no longer.

" I did not hope to see you before to-
morrow," she said, looking up in his face with
a timid smile.

" Very probably," returned Ogilvie drily,
" I only arrived this morning, having caught
the night mail at Greystone and after a busy
day; I made a push to see you before dinner,
as I am dining out."

" It is very good of you to come, but you
are always good."

" Thank you," still in the same dry tone.
" Pray how is it that Carr made his way
here?" turning suddenly to her with searching
angry eyes, while the light from the gas-
brackets at either side of the mantelpiece fell

upon his face, and showed the set, displeased
expression that contracted his brow.

" Why Madame Falk must have given him
my address when she asked him to take the
parcel, but he forgot to bring it on Monday—
so——"

" He was here on Monday too! Why did
you not let me know ? "

" If I had written to you I should certainly
have mentioned it, but I never thought of
troubling you with a letter merely to say that.
Some time ago, when Madame Falk told me
he was going to Audeley Chase, I repeated it
to you."

" At all events, Carr evidently knew how
to make his second visit fit in with Miss
Macallan's rather unusual absence from the
house."

" But, Mr. Ogilvie, he could have known
nothing about it! Miss Macallan had arranged
to pay her visit to Hampstead before I had Mr.
Carr's note, saying he could come to-day."

" Ha! He wrote to make the appoint-
ment then ? "

" Yes, I asked him to write. I should have

been so vexed to miss him. Why do you question me in this strange way? Why are you displeased?"

There was a degree of quiet dignity in May's look and manner which recalled Ogilvie to common-sense and self-control.

"Forgive me, May," he said, walking towards the door and back again. "I have been hasty, perhaps, but an inexperienced girl like yourself, especially one so divested of natural protectors, needs to be extra careful of her conduct, and—and of the sort of men she admits to her intimacy. I do not mean to say that Carr is a bad man, as men go, but I don't want him to boast that you received him alone!"

"Mr. Carr boast of being received by *me!*" repeated May, with a natural, unaffected laugh. "I hope he will have some better reason for boasting—if he ever boasts—which I do not think he does."

"You have a high opinion of Carr?" returned Ogilvie, leaning his shoulder against the end of the mantelshelf, and fixing his eyes on hers as if he would read her thoughts.

May met them fully; the suspicion they expressed nerved her to bear his gaze, as she could not have done had they questioned her tenderly.

" I do not know Mr. Carr well enough to have any distinct opinion about him, but he is nice and kind, and has a pleasant, frank, youthful air that I like, but probably I shall never see him again."

" Why not? he will no doubt return to London, and equally without doubt call upon you."

" I do not think he will, when you have so plainly shown him that you do not wish it."

" Did I?" said Ogilvie, amazed at the composure of her tone. " Well, I do *not* wish him to come here—it is much better he should not. A man like him, accustomed to indulge in every whim, with a huge fortune, it is incongruous, it is unfit."

" Why?" asked May very quietly. " What are his whims or his fortune to me? I only know him as a friendly stranger, who can never go out of my life because he never came into it! Why do you trouble yourself about him ? If you think it worth while to ask me not to receive Mr. Carr, I will not see him. I do not care to vex my best friend for the sake of a mere acquaintance, only I will *not* be rude to him."

Ogilvie paused before he replied. He had rarely felt so annoyed with himself. He felt he had made a mistake, and shown his hand dangerously at least; had May been more experienced and worldly she would have seen a good deal too much.

" Thank you, my dear ward, for the confidence you show in me ; I think I deserve it," he said, at length, in a deliberate voice. " You must remember there are many social matters which men understand better than women, even experienced women, which you cannot claim to be! Yes, May, I believe I am your best friend. I do not think any one else takes the profound interest in you that I do ; give me your complete trust in return, I ask no more."

" You have it—you know you have," murmured May ; there was a tremor in her voice that sent a thrill through his veins.

Last week she would have seconded her words by holding out her hand to him, to-day something forbade the action.

But Ogilvie settled the matter by taking the chill little hand in one of his, and then laying the other over it. "You are cold," he said, pressing it closely and tenderly, "and I have annoyed you; you think me suspicious and ill-tempered."

"I think you are unjust," she said, "but it is not of much consequence; only do not be cross again, it makes me unhappy."

A quick, deep sigh heaved Ogilvie's breast. "God knows, I only ask to make you happy," he said in a low tone.

"Well, so far, you have succeeded," she returned, with a smiling upward glance, as she gently withdrew her hand.

"Now," she resumed, "tell me of your visit to the great man; "is Lord Shelbourne going to send you to the ends of the earth?"

"Well, no—nor should I have gone if he had. I would rather quit the service than quit England just now. I have a good deal of work before me. The government has got hold of a lot of papers in Russian which may be of importance—so instead of giving them to the ordinary interpreters I am to have the honour of deciphering and translating them. There—there is another state secret for you to keep. You see you had better know as little as possible of me and my movements."

" I never do ! " said May, while her heart beat fast as the question arose in her mind, " Can it be possible that he stays in England for my sake ? " and this possibility sent a wave of roseate colour for one fleeting moment over Life in all its aspects.

" No ! " returned Ogilvie. " I know you do not. A woman—I prefer calling you a woman, young as you are—a woman who is absolutely safe, and there are some, though they are rare, is the most delicious friend in the world—and the most useful."

" I should like to play mouse to your lion in the toils, though not even for that gratification would I wish you to be in difficulties," said May, who was once more at her ease and happy.

Ogilvie did not reply.

May, who had taken up some needlework, plied her needle in silence.

" I suppose Miss Macallan would think me very remiss if I did not come to see her to-morrow ? "

" I am sure she would."

" Then I will come after luncheon, and afterwards, if it is fine, we—we will go some where. Then I must hear you sing—for— " looking at his watch, " I must go back to every-day life." A little more talk of the Conroys and what Mr. Conroy had said of his wife's health when Ogilvie had met him that morning in Whitehall, and he took his leave.

" We are as fast friends as ever, are we not May ? You forgive me for fancying you had any leaven of that infernal coquetry which degrades and destroys most women ? "

" I forgive you certainly. But whether I have any coquetry in me neither you nor I know. It has never been called forth."

" Do you know you sometimes startle me by suggesting that I by no means know you thoroughly yet."

" Well, I think you do. Good-bye till to-morrow."

It was a dry, clear evening, and Ogilvie walked quickly towards town, as no hansom presented itself for some little time. He was glad of a few minutes' thought to examine his position, for he had been profoundly mortified by his own sudden failure under fire, as he considered his loss of self-control. And for what ? He now felt convinced that May was also absolutely innocent of any coquetry or design as regarded Carr. What a fool he had made of himself!

" I have staked more than I intended on this game," he said to himself, " but it is intensely interesting. How I am ever to do without this tender shadowy 'friendship' I don't exactly see. Yet the whole affair bristles with difficulties. May is no common-place woman. I doubt if any one save herself can throw dust in her eyes. Will she play Dust-man in my favour ? I dare not make love to her *yet*, and she seems perfectly content with the Dummy of friendship. Until I feel sure that she *is* in love with me, I dare not show

my hand, even if she is—and with all my
experience I cannot tell—it will not be an
easy task to bring her into my views. This
infernal good-looking bushranger turning up
too! It was enough to unsteady any man's
nerve to see him bending over her, and think
of his advantages! Young, wealthy, un-
dazzled by European life, with his quixotic
ideas, he is quite capable of marrying her,
and carrying her off to a soul-less life among
the kangaroos. But love or no love, I think
I have influence enough to stop that. Well,
patience and coolness shall carry the day, or
I am much mistaken." Here an empty
hansom came up ; Ogilvie hailed it, jumped
in and rolled away to his rooms in Duke
Street.

This momentary sprinkling on the glowing
warmth of their friendship seemed to have
only served to draw May and her guardian
closer. Time sped on tranquilly and happily.

If Ogilvie came less frequently to Granby
Road he managed to stay longer when he did
come. He seemed to have more orders for
private boxes than ever.

The Conroys were for two days in town, about the middle of December, two days which May passed almost completely with Frances and her mother, finding both as kind and interested in herself as ever, and Frances more sympathetic than May had ever known her before.

Mrs. Conroy, though anxious to get some warm, sunny, winter place, was not worse than usual, and both mother and daughter spoke cheerfully of returning in the spring and taking May back with them to the Chase.

Both deeply regretted that Ogilvie had been obliged to run down to Yorkshire for a couple of days just when they came to town.

It was a rush altogether that brief spell of intercourse, and May felt terribly lonely when she had bid them good-bye at Charing Cross and returned to the desolate rigidity of Miss Macallan's solidly-furnished dwelling.

But the day after Ogilvie appeared in the evening, and made himself delightfully agreeable both to May and to Miss Macallan, after which came a spell of peaceful monotony, which to May was anything but monotonous.

Meanwhile the Fates spun diligently the humble web of May's destiny, intertwining many side issues in its meshes.

＊　　＊　　＊　　＊　　＊

Carr did not return directly to Paris. He found an Australian friend who persuaded him to run down to Torquay, and it was not till after a short stay there that Carr made his way across the Channel.

Madame Falk had had only one short letter from May since Carr's visit to her. In this she expressed her great pleasure at seeing him, and thanked her kind friend for her useful present of gloves.

Busy as she was Madame Falk had had no time to answer, or even to wonder at Carr's silence, though he had promised to write, and this particular afternoon on which the story returns to her, her pen was galloping at hot speed towards the end of a letter to be finished and despatched by five o'clock. Absorbed though she was, her attention was caught by voices in the vestibule.

" But Madame is occupied, Monsieur, I

must not disturb her," she heard Adrienne say in firm accents.

"Miss Barton, then?" returned a male voice.

"Is gone out, Monsieur."

"May I sit down and wait?"

"Yes, of course you can!" cried Madame Falk, bursting out upon the interlocutors. "My dear Mr. Carr, if you will wait twenty minutes in the *salon* without a fire, I shall be quite free. Here are cigarettes, and papers, and books. I am dying to talk to you, but I *must* get my letter off first—no, keep on your overcoat."

"And I am dying to talk to you! Yes! of course I will wait."

Madame Falk opened the door of the *salon*, thrust Carr into it, and retired to her own den, almost before he had finished speaking.

Carr waited patiently; he smoked two or three cigarettes, skimmed three or four papers, and had looked at the title-page of a yellow-covered novel, when Madame Falk's cheery, pleasant voice called to him from the inner room:

31*

" You must be cold!—if you don't mind a scene of confusion, come in here."

Carr obeyed.

" I was well used to confusion once," he said, smiling, as he drew a chair facing Madame Falk. " I hadn't the luck to be brought up with any women about me. I don't remember my mother, I fancy it is a great loss, makes a fellow rather rugged."

" You are not rugged," she returned, as she tied up and sealed her packet. " Here, Adrienne," to the *bonne*, who came in obedience to her hand-bell. " Take this to the post at once. Now, thank Heaven, I am free for the rest of the day, and can enjoy a good long gossip, if you will so far indulge me."

" You cannot enjoy it more than I shall; I suppose you want to hear all about Miss Riddell? First of all, here is a parcel for you," and he presented one done up in brown paper. " It has been in my portmanteau for more than a fortnight."

Madame Falk thanked him and laid it aside.

" I found the young lady looking remarkably well, in fact I did not think her pretty
before ; nor is she exactly pretty, but there is
something charming in her face, something
uncommon, and by Jove! what expressive
eyes she has! She was uncommonly pleased
to see me. Oh! I am not conceited," for
Madame Falk smiled, "I don't suppose it was
for my own sake, but to talk about you and
Miss Barton, and a little woman I have seen
here."

" I know—Mademoiselle Perret," put in
Madame Falk.

" Then the lady she is living with came in,
which was a great nuisance," continued Carr,
" for we were getting on splendidly. Miss
Riddell is less shy, less silent than she used to
be, and I felt quite at home with her. This
lady, a Miss Macallan, seems a formidable
female ; she is head and shoulders over you,
and has not an ounce of unnecessary flesh,
she has a sort of iron jaw and high cheek-
bones—altogether a hard, obstinate-looking
woman, with a voice to match. It seems she's
a relation of Ogilvie, and from the way she

talked you could see that she considers him the biggest man living."

" I am afraid poor dear May cannot be happy or comfortable with such a woman ! " exclaimed Madame Falk.

" She's not *un*happy, I feel sure," returned Carr, with a far-away look in his eyes, as if he were conjuring up May's face before him.

" No, she is not unhappy, and I don't think that dour-looking employer of hers would venture to offend a *protégée* of Ogilvie's—but she'd like to be living with you. The house she is in is dull and square and bare, though it is handsomely furnished, but the only pleasant-looking thing in it (after Miss Riddell herself) is a rosy-cheeked young servant. The old lady was fairly civil, and dying to know all about me."

" It must be most depressing to May to live in such a house," ejaculated Madame Falk. " I must persuade her to take a holiday and come over to us."

" Yes, do, Madame Falk ! " he cried. I wanted her to come back with me, but——"

"Of course she would not," she interrupted. "It would not do, here at least."

"Then I had another talk with her, I forgot your package the first time, so I went again. The old Gorgon was out, and I was shown up to the drawing-room. It is a trifle less ghastly than the *salle-à-manger*. Then there was a piano and a good fire, so we talked at a great pace —anyway I did—and she sang me a song without any fuss or trouble, and very sweetly she sang. It seems Ogilvie wishes her to learn, that she may teach hereafter if necessary."

"Very considerate of him," remarked Madame Falk.

"Perhaps," returned Carr in rather a discontented tone. "I don't know how it is, but I never liked Ogilvie ; there is something inscrutable about him."

"Well, yes, a little—but I must say he has been so wonderfully kind about May, not at all what one could have expected."

"I had just gone over to the piano to ask for another song, when the door opened and

Ogilvie came in, stopping for half a second, looking as black as thunder."

" Why ? " asked Madame Falk, opening her eyes.

" Because he found me there ! "

" Oh ! impossible."

" I only know he gave me a flash of ·his eyes, that might have been followed by a spring at my throat from their expression—I only wish he'd have tried it!! Of course it was a mere lightning glimpse of hell !—then he was as cool and polite as ever, and made suitable conversation with great ease, but he hardly noticed Miss Riddell, and she did not seem quite at her ease. Then when I offered to call again for your little packet there, he said it would be sent to me, in a tone which forbade me to return. I am pretty sure he rules that nice young creature with a rod of iron."

" My dear Mr. Carr, you exaggerate ! May is quite fond of him."

" She may be, but the little scene made a deucedly unpleasant impression on me, and things I have heard said have come back to my mind."

" What things ? " interrupted Madame Falk. " Against Ogilvie ? "

" No ; not against anyone in particular, but I wish you would ask May Riddell to come and stay with you, she would be better with you than with anyone else."

" I should greatly like to have her, and to treat her as a daughter, but, Mr. Carr, she would never consent to live on my bounty, and without any special training it would be long before she could find such remunerative employment here as she has in London, and it would not be wise to disoblige Mr. Ogilvie."

" You have all let Ogilvie get too tight a grip of you," cried Carr impatiently, then unconsciously taking a sheet of scribbled paper, he began to fold it and unfold it with long, bony, brown hands. " There need be no difficulty about Miss Riddell coming to stay with you," he said nervously, and looking away from his interlocutor.

" More than you think," she returned. " I am quite sure May would not quit London without Mr. Ogilvie's full permission."

" What ? " said Carr, throwing away his

paper and gazing at Madame Falk with earnest, questioning eyes. "Do you think he has acquired such influence over her?"

"That is not exactly the way to put it. She certainly owes him some degree of deference to his wishes, considering all he has done for her. You seem very much impressed by your meeting with Mr. Ogilvie—tell me what you fear? You have made me quite uncomfortable."

"What I fear?" he repeated slowly, "I scarcely know. It is a sort of dim distrust— a kind of, perhaps unreasonable, conviction that this guardianship business will not end happily for May—I mean Miss Riddell——" He stopped.

"You are speaking out all you think you foresee," said Madame Falk thoughtfully. "But I fancy I can understand you, and I do not think you are right. Ogilvie is a cool-headed man of the world—entirely taken up with ambition and business. It has chanced that, being accidentally present at Mr. Riddell's death, he is struck and touched by the sad position of the desolate orphan—and

the sensation of pity is new and interesting—
so he befriends her ; but he will be sent somewhere, or marry. May will find employment,
perhaps near me, and the present tie between
them will wear away, leaving only a kindly
memory behind. But I am personally gratified
by your friendly interest in my dear young
friend."

" Yes, she interests me ! "

" I tell you what I will do," resumed
Madame Falk. " I will ask her to pay me a
visit before Easter, fixing the date and making
a point of ,it. She will come, I am sure, and
I shall learn more from her own lips than
from anything else."

" I hope you may. Yes, *do* ask her. I
shall be in Paris then, I think, and we'll have
some Coroberries ! "

" Some what ? " repeated Madame Falk.

" Coroberries—Australian for ' high jinks.' "

" Thank you. And did you see Mr.
Conroy and Frances ? "

" No. They were away in the South of
England. Audeley Chase is a delightful
house—an ideal English country home.

When shall we have anything like it in Australia?"

" Pray, remember how many centuries it took to create English homes."

" True. Then we started half-way!"

" Yes, but you carried weight, in the shape of new and difficult conditions."

" Yes, and we must develop on different lines."

" Nothing can be secured without paying a price," concluded Madame Falk, who had been "sorting" her papers while she spoke.

" I fear I have trespassed too long," said Carr, riring.

" By no means. I have been deeply interested in all you have said."

" And you will be sure to ask Miss Riddell over in February or March?"

" You may be sure I shall. I am a good deal more anxious to see her than you can be."

" Will you and Miss Barton do me the honour of dining with me at the Café Bignon any day that suits you?"

" Many thanks. We shall be very pleased."

" I will call to-morrow to learn what date you have fixed."

They shook hands, and Carr turned to leave the room. As he did so he was face to face with the two photographs which hung opposite Madame Falk's accustomed seat.

The light from the window which partially faced them showed them clearly, for it was still early afternoon on a bright, clear day. Carr stopped short, his eyes fixed on the portrait of the man.

" Who is that ? " he asked abruptly. His voice showed that he was moved to forgetfulness of conventional etiquette.

" That," said Madame Falk, in a low tone, and pausing after the first word, " is the likeness of my late husband."

" Your husband ! " cried Carr. " That cannot be ! It is the portrait—it must be the portrait of my father, only younger looking than I remember him twenty years ago ! "

" For Heaven's sake ! " said Madame Falk, in a distressed voice, " do not tear open old wounds ! That is my poor husband as he was a year before I lost him."

" And to me it seems as certainly my father, whom I vividly remember, for I was his constant companion till I was ten years old, when he died.   What does it all mean?"

" It is an accidental likeness. It can be nothing more," said Madame Falk. " My husband was lost at sea. He never reached land. There can be no connection between his portrait and the father you remember." She sat down as she spoke, and to her own surprise found herself trembling from head to foot.

CHAPTER IX

CARR was greatly upset by the evident emotion of Madame Falk. It seemed cruel and ill-bred to press any enquiries upon her—yet he was burning for further information.

"Pray forgive me, for disturbing you," he said. "I fear it must seem intrusive on my part questioning you about your pictures, but I was so startled, so struck by the likeness I recognised, that the words had passed my lips before I could stop them. If it distresses you I shall say no more, perhaps some other day you will allow me——"

"Ah, no!" she interrupted. "Let the dead past bury its dead. I do not wish to think that picture can by any possibility resemble your father—strange that at this distance of time the old pain should thrill me. No—my dear young friend—let us not speak on this matter again — it would do you no

good—on the contrary it might open your
eyes to possible wrong and sorrow if the
portrait proved to be that of your father.
No, Mr. Carr, do not speak of it again."

"I will of course obey you!" he said slowly
—his eyes fixed on the photograph. "I will
leave you now. But do not punish my
thoughtless out-spokenness by forbidding me
to come again!"

"No—I should be sorry to lose the
pleasure of seeing you!" said Madame Falk
kindly and cordially, "though I will let you
go now, and you may be sure I shall write to
May and settle about her coming here. You
have made me just a little uncomfortable about
Ogilvie, unnecessarily so I am sure." She
spoke more in her usual tone, but evidently
by an effort. Carr therefore shook hands
cordially with her and went away—descend-
ing the stairs slowly and thoughtfully.

"It is all very curious," he thought, for he
too had been deeply moved by the sight of
his father's well-remembered features. He
had been passionately attached to the only
parent he had ever known—and had had a

strange lonely boyhood, the only companion
of a gloomy, irritable man, who was rough
and stern to everyone save his son. His early
recollections presented him with a picture of
wild open-air life, among horses and cattle,
hills and pasture. His home was a rude log-
hut on a farm or ranche—at some distance
from a cluster of buildings of the same description only larger and better. This farm
was not his father's. The "Boss" was an
older man, rough and masterful too, but his
roughness was more rugged than course. His
father was a man of some importance nevertheless, and often went away with the Boss on
expeditions, and held long discussions with
him.

The Boss had a wife who seemed to Carr
very old, in those childish days, but there
were no children to play with him. The Lady
Boss was wonderfully good to him and made
cakes and pies for his delectation, and was
always wanting him to stay with her—yet he
was an ungrateful toad and did not care to be
with his benefactress. His greatest pleasure
was to have lessons with his father, who in

the winter evenings taught him regularly. Then came bad times, disease got among the cattle, and fever seized the men.

Among them, Carr's father. He was terribly ill and delirious and then—the child had no father!

The Boss and his wife were very good to him. He became their son. By-and-by they broke up their establishment—things were all going wrong. Then various pictures came out of memory's store-house, more or less blurred and faded by the fanning of Time's sombre pinions. A big city — a glorious panorama of mountain and sea. Long days on board ship—delightful sailors who let him skin his hands playing with rough tarry ropes —the grandeur of wide ocean raging under the scourge of the storm-fiend—such were the pictures which swept over Carr's mental field of vision, as he wandered through the streets of Paris, that beautiful city, perhaps the most graceful product of civilisation in Europe. He had not thought of his early rough life for many a day, and now, that photograph had brought it all before his eyes so freshly.

He must—he would—find out all about it, yet he did not want to annoy Madame Falk or cause her pain.

The expression of her face as she begged him not to open old wounds came back to him. It expressed infinite sorrow.

He had a great regard for Madame Falk. There was a tone of wholesome strength—of sound common sense—in her air and conversation that made her a most agreeable companion to Carr. He had profound faith in the loyalty of her nature and would have (he knew not why) have trusted his life to her simple promise. No, he would not pain or annoy her, but he would find out something about that picture—he must, he could not rest till he had. But how? Looking round for ways and means to carry out this determination he thought of Miss Barton.

Of this lady he had not quite so high an opinion as of her cousin and partner—she amused him, however, and he shrewdly surmised that profit of any kind was not without its importance in her eyes. It would, however, be shabby to pump her behind Madame Falk's back, yet the matter was very important to him—suppose he turned out some relation to them? suppose—(his brown cheek flushed) suppose his father had deserted Madame Falk, and married his (Carr's) mother under some other name? True his present appellation was that of the friendly Boss who had adopted him, he scarcely knew what his own had been, he rather believed it had been the same as his own Christian name. It was all very puzzling. Would it not be better to leave it alone, rather than unravel the mystery only to find the bar sinister on his scutcheon? He would wait and see.

At this point in his reflections his progress was arrested by M. Dupont, who greeted him cordially, and informed him that Madame Zavadoskoï had arrived in Paris for the winter, and poured forth many enquiries for their mutual friends. He himself had been in America — had enjoyed his visit — but—Heavens! how good it was to be once more in the city of cities.

Having taken a turn with him on the Boulevards, Carr called a *fiacre*—and went away to leave his card on Madame Zavadoskoï.

On her side Madame Falk had been greatly shaken by Carr's abrupt questions — not that she believed there was more than an accidental resemblance between her lost husband's picture and the young man's father.

She was generally successful in keeping bitter memories at bay. To *her*, defeat and unhappiness meant destruction—she could not fret and live! Hope was strong within her. Hope had kept her up at first under her cruel trials, and then just indignation had flamed out to keep the springs of her vitality warm and in motion. Time brought many new lights by which to view her husband's conduct; her final conviction being that, for the moment, fierce jealousy had destroyed the balance of his reason, and, before he could recover it, "he had gone down into the grave where all things are forgotten"; and her sweet boy, ah! it was too cruel to rob her of him! that was the strongest proof of temporary insanity. She thanked God for this belief, which brought her that blessed balm—the power to forgive! Was it—could it be possible, that her half-insane husband, escaping the perils of the deep, to which his baby-boy had probably succumbed, had found another companion—the mother of Carr?—that he was right in his recognition? The idea did not rouse in her any indignation. It was so long ago—quite five-and-twenty years—that it all seemed to have happened in another life. *If* he had lived—it was not improbable that he had formed some such connection. But these were dreams—mere dreams.

By the time Miss Barton had returned to dinner Madame Falk was quite herself, though the sharp eyes of her loving, but domineering, friend detected something not exactly normal in her looks.

" What's the matter, Esther? You are as white as paper, and your eyes are quite dark underneath. Have you had a touch of neuralgia, hey?" she asked as she sent away her soup-plate.

" No, nothing whatever. I have been fairly free from that fiend, neuralgia, this winter.

Will you take some *Lapin en gibelotte* or *rognons?*" And the comfortable little dinner went on, interspersed with scraps of talk and bits of gossips.

After a pause of some duration—as Adrienne carried away the last dish, and as Madame Falk handed the roast chestnuts to her cousin, she said :

"Mr. Carr paid me a long visit to-day. He told me all about May, who seems very well placed—by the way, how old would you take Carr to be ?"

"Well—let me see. He is old-looking for twenty-five, or young-looking for twenty-seven; I am sure he is not twenty-eight."

"I should not think him so much ; but you are a better judge than I am, Sarah."

"I don't know. There is something boyish about him. Then, anyone may be boyish when they are free from care, as he is, lucky fellow ! And what report did he give of May ?"

"A very good one. She is living with one of those rich, eccentric old maids, who seem to abound in England, and who is very fond

of her, still it must be a dull life. He met
Mr. Ogilvie, who is some relative to this Miss
Macallan. I don't think he likes Ogilvie."

"No? Why doesn't he like him, Esther?"

"I cannot tell; but he is disposed to think
that Ogilvie exercises too much authority or
influence, or both, over May."

"Oh, pooh, nonsense!"—a pause—then
abruptly: "I say, Esther, do you think Mr.
Carr has any fancy for our young friend?"

"No; certainly not. I wish, Sarah, you
would not allow yourself to think in such a
common-place groove. I hate that tendency
to fancy all young men and women not all
in love with each other."

"Well, they very often do."

"At all events, I do not think Mr. Carr is
inclined that way. He is kind and friendly,
that is all."

"All I can say, Esther, I wish it were a
little more. Just think what a match it
would be for May!"

"I am going to ask her here for the Easter
Holidays, and mind, Sarah, you never let a
syllable drop that could suggest such an idea

to May. Carr will look for some distinguished beauty, you know almost anyone would accept him."

" My dear Esther, I am not quite an idiot."

" I don't suppose you are. But wise people sometimes do foolish things. By-the-way, Mr. Carr wishes to give us a dinner at some café, it will be very pleasant."

To this Miss Barton assented, and then the partners turned to their usual evening occupations, occasionally exchanging a few words, which proved how much they regretted the absence of May, whose company was peculiarly valuable in the long winter evenings.

Madame Falk confessed to herself that she was rather curious to know if Carr would return, and endeavour to reassume his former footing, or would show something of wounded pride at the abrupt rejection of his ideas touching the likeness to his father in the late Falk.

A few days, however, settled the question.

Mr. Carr called, but no one was at home. The evening post brought a very polite note,

asking Madame Falk to name a day on
which she and Miss Barton would do him the
favour of dining with him. This invitation
was at once accepted, and Carr himself came
to conduct them to his hotel, where he finally
decided to give the entertainment ; a couple
of well-known artists, the correspondent of a
leading English paper, and an African ex-
plorer, were the male guests. A favourite
American poetess was the third lady.   It
was a pleasant gathering. Many were the
theories started and discussed. Orthodoxy
would have wrapped its face in its dinner-
napkin had it been present—but it had no re-
presentative—and the conversation boxed the
compass of subjects more or less forbidden.

It was a symposium such as Madame Falk
thoroughly enjoyed, and she was one of the
most brilliant talkers.

Carr found an opportunity of speaking
aside with Miss Barton, while the whole party
were arguing eagerly respecting the impres-
sionist school, then in its infancy.

" I should like so much to have a little
private talk with you, Miss Barton," he said.

" I want you to be so good as to solve a riddle for me."

" A riddle ? I don't fancy I can be of much use to you in solving a riddle."

" But you will not refuse to try ? Moreover, it must be a profound secret, even from Madame Falk."

" I can be secret enough," returned Miss Barton, whose curiosity began to wake up.

" Then, where can I see you alone ? "

" Ah, you are a wicked young man to tempt a woman of my years and discretion to grant you a rendezvous. Let me see—Monday—Madame Falk is generally out all day. Call on Monday about two. I am beginning to be consumed with unholy eagerness to know what the secret is about. I suppose there is a woman in it ? "

" Yes, it is chiefly about a woman."

" Hum—young and charming ? "

" Very charming."

" Who can it be ? I know no very charming woman except Madame Zavadoskoï ? "

" No, it is not the fascinating Russian. You shall know everything on Monday."

" So for four days I am to suffer the pangs of unsatisfied curiosity ? "

" Yes, I fear you must. And not a word to Madame Falk."

Here Carr was summoned by the poetess, who thought he had spent time enough on that ugly old woman.

The intervening days, which Miss Barton affected to dread as too severe a trial of patience, went by in the usual way, Madame Falk being even more than ever engrossed in her work, but her observant kinswoman noticed that she was silent and even depressed ; but that was a mere passing mood, Miss Barton decided, and so allowed her mind to dwell on the triumph which awaited her prophetic discrimination, for she had quite convinced herself that the secret to be imparted to her by the gay, genial Australian related to his new fancy for May. Somehow or other Esther must have thrown cold water on his dawning passion.

" Like a fool as she is in certain directions, with all her cleverness," mused Sarah. " Instead of encouraging him with all her might.

Why it would be a good thing for us all if he married May! What does he make a hubble about I cannot imagine! Rich and free, and pleasant-looking if not regularly handsome, of course May would jump at him, though she is rather cold ; I doubt if she would ever care much about anyone. There is no reason in the world why he should hold back, if he isn't already married to some squaw out in Australia—no, they are not squaws there— some bushranger's daughter, or—well, men *are* idiots—they are either shy or audacious, but always in the wrong direction. It will be a great marriage for May (that is if Carr is not already married). It is certainly about her, and Esther will have to confess that I can see an inch or two further through a mill-stone than she can—well, we'll see."

The eagerly anticipated Monday arrived at last. Madame Falk hurried away after luncheon, with a long list of things to be seen, and places to call at, and Miss Barton changed her morning gown for her best garment of black silk and jet, with a fine

cravatte of white Brussels lace, in honour of
the expected visit from her " young man."

Carr presented himself punctually at two
o'clock.

" It is very good of you to receive me!" he
said as they shook hands.

" My dear sir ! I have been counting the
minutes till you came !"

" I confess I have come with the meanest
intentions—to pump you on more than one
point. Have you any idea what about ?"

" Well, perhaps I have. You see I am
neither a bat nor a mole."

" Ah! Then Madame Falk has told you
how disturbed she was by my recognition of
the photograph ?"

" Recognition of the photograph ?—no—
not a word—what *do* you mean ?"

" It is understood that all we say is under
the seal of secrecy. Though I am the person
chiefly concerned, I would not vex Madame
Falk for the world, nor do her any harm for
two or three."

" All right, Mr. Carr, I'll be as secret as the
grave. Get on, do."

" When I was here last week Madame Falk let me come into her workshop—or study— and there my eye was caught by a photograph that startled me by its resemblance to my poor father, who has been dead more than twenty years. I noticed it to Madame Falk, and to my regret and confusion she was greatly upset, so I did not pursue the subject. I hope it is not wrong or mean of me to come and pump you, but I cannot rest till I know a little more about the husband whose portrait Madame Falk said it was."

" No, why should it be wrong? I know my cousin cannot bear to speak of the past, but there is nothing in it for her to be ashamed of, and it doesn't hurt *me* to talk of it."

" Thank you, Miss Barton, and pray remember I have heard some outline of her story already from Madame Zavadoskoï. This has suggested some strange ideas, I may say hopes. Now let me see that picture again."

" Certainly."

Miss Barton rose, and opened the door into her cousin's den. Carr followed, and gazed long and steadily at the photograph.

"And this one?" he asked, pointing to that of the child.

"That is the little boy who was lost with him."

"Ah! well a likeness at that age does not count," observed Carr. "The longer I look at that picture the more convinced I am that it represents my father, only younger than I remember him. There is the same turn of the head, and curve of the jaw! I wish his left ear were not hidden."

"Why?"

"Oh, because it had a curious natural defect at the top, in the hem of the ear there was a little triangular nip, as if it had been bitten by some animal. Do you remember anything of that kind about this man whom you call Falk?"

Miss Barton shook her head.

"No, I do not, but I saw very little of him. He was a crazy savage, and nearly cost my poor dear cousin her life. No one *could* understand the agony she went through who had not seen it. God forgive him!"

"Hush!" said Carr, a look of pain contracting his open countenance. "Will you tell me," he resumed, after a moment's pause, "how long is it since—since Madame Falk was—that is lost—her husband and boy?"

"About twenty-six years."

"How old was the boy?"

"Just five, I think."

"Then if he were alive he would be thirty-one?"

"Of course!"

"Pray, Miss Barton, tell me the story—your version of it; what I heard is very sketchy."

Miss Barton complied, wondering what it was to lead to.

"Then you never had a trace of them after the shipwreck?" he asked, when she paused in the narrative, to which he had listened with rapt attention.

"Never. Some of the passengers who escaped described Falk getting into a boat with the child in his arms, but that boat was lost, at least none of those who were in it ever appeared again."

"Twenty-six years ago," repeated Carr, as if to himself.

"Yes, a little more than twenty-six years. But if you were Falk's son, how is it you are called Carr?"

"Because I took the name of the man who adopted me. My father's name, and my own first name now, is Bernard!"

"Bernard!" repeated Miss Barton in a high key of extreme astonishment. "Why that was Falk's name! Bernard Falk! This is startling."

"My father," continued Carr, "was a German, that was one tie with the Carrs; Mrs. Carr was German, and never spoke English without difficulty; she used to have long talks with my father in their own tongue, and tended him in his last illness— my oldest, far-away, dream-like memory is being hugged up to my father's breast, the cold howling wind, and great dark green waves raging round—of being wet through. Then I can remember nothing till we were among woods and hills, and my good friends the Carrs were mixed up with my life."

And he proceeded to give a sketch of his existence, which has been already presented.

"After I went with my friends to Australia, Mrs. Carr died, some years before her husband," concluded the young man. "He was a rugged and uncultivated Scotsman, not ignorant; a fine character, who fought hard with circumstances, and was on the eve of conquering them when death took him. He left me all he had, and I worked on, on his lines, when gold was discovered on my property, and my fortune was made — no thanks to me! According to my father's reckoning, when he was alive, I was thirty last May; put all this together, Miss Barton, and say—Have I not a right to believe, to hope, that Madame Falk is my mother? If so, by God's help, I will be a good son, and in some degree atone for my poor unhappy father's cruel mistake, the terrible wrong he inflicted on her."

"It's as plain as the nose on your face!" cried Miss Barton enthusiastically. "My dear young kinsman, *I* accept you with all my heart!" and she held out both hands to him.

"Thank you!" returned Carr, grasping them cordially, while his soft brown eyes lit up with pleasure. " But — I am afraid Madame Falk will want a lot of proof, and even if she is convinced, how will she like the son of my father ? "

" How will she like her own son, you mean ? Why she'll make a fool of herself about you, as most mothers do, I am pretty sure! Leave it all to me! It is the most wonderful, the most romantic story I ever heard in my life ! "

" And when will you speak to her ? "

" Oh—on the first opportunity—and have you anything in your father's writing that might convince her ? "

" The only thing belonging to him I possess is a small volume of poetry with a line or two of writing on the title page, and some pencil sketches—but I haven't them with me."

" Then send for them, like a dear!" cried Miss Barton, effusively—she was in such a

state of excitement she scarcely knew what
she was saying. Not only did she think Carr
a delightful young man—but she felt as if
that vein of gold of which he had spoken had
been suddenly deflected across land and sea
to touch the very small pile her cousin and
herself had contrived to accumulate, with its
multiplying power.

"Yes! send for them! You see Madame
Falk, I mean your mother—for *I* am quite
convinced she is—has peculiar notions, and is
greatly troubled with a tiresome conscience,
so we must leave nothing undone to convince
her——"

"Certainly not!" returned Carr—adding in
a graver tone, "and though I might perhaps
have been steadier than I've been, I don't
think she need be ashamed of me."

"I am sure not!—and she—ah—my dear
young friend, you may well be proud of *her*
—she *is* a good woman—I am a greedy,
selfish old heathen compared to her. If you
were in rags and tatters—once she believed
you were hers—she'd take you to her warm
heart!—while I—I don't deny it, may be

influenced by that gold you mentioned!
Despise me or not — there's the truth for
you!"

"It's a sort of truth very few would have
the courage to speak," said Carr laughing.
"I certainly do not despise you for it!"

"Now, my dear boy, you just go away, I
want to have time to compose myself and
arrange my plan of proceeding before she
comes in. I will write to you to-morrow,
whatever happens."

"Pray do—I shall be awfully anxious! I
think there can be no doubt—and the book
may be valuable evidence, so good-bye, and
many many thanks for your friendly sympathy!" With a hearty hand-shake they
parted company—and Miss Barton plumped
down on the sofa.

"Yes—I am sympathetic—and truly so,
but I am a mercenary old sinner into the
bargain! My poor Esther! who has worked
so hard and battled so gallantly!—to think
that she will have a fine son—a *rich* son to
stand by her when age and incapacity come.
I do hope and pray that she will not let any

crotchets get the better of her. She shan't
—she mustn't!"

When Madame Falk came in, very tired
and rather damp—for the evening turned out
wet, and she had forgotten her umbrella—
she found everything tidied up, and in a high
state of readiness.

"Why, Sarah," she exclaimed, as they sat
down to dinner, "what has happened? You
have quite a colour—I hope you haven't a
touch of toothache?"

"Oh, dear no! I stood a while in the
kitchen making a mayonnaise and the fire
caught my face."

Madame Falk went on to describe some
pictures she had seen in the artist's studies
she had visited — Miss Barton was a little
distrait — finally the conversation dragged
somewhat.

"Esther!" said her cousin after a short
pause, "I want to ask you a question—and I
am half afraid."

"Nonsense, Sarah! what is it?"

"It's—it's about him," nodding her curly
grey head in the direction of the Den.

Madame Falk understood.

"Speak then," she said, with a quick sigh.

"Tell me, Esther — had he—had he any-thing—any mark on his left ear?"

"What can have put that into your head, Sarah?" exclaimed Madame Falk, greatly surprised. "Yes, he had a curious mark— as if a tiny bit had been pinched out at the edge."

"Then," cried Miss Barton, standing up in her excitement, " as sure as you sit there young Carr is your son."

END OF VOL. II.